Jana ♡

Give me some

Ruff Love!

Also by Karina Halle

The Experiment in Terror Series

Darkhouse (EIT #1)
Red Fox (EIT #2)
The Benson (EIT #2.5)
Dead Sky Morning (EIT #3)
Lying Season (EIT #4)
On Demon Wings (EIT #5)
Old Blood (EIT #5.5)
The Dex-Files (EIT #5.7)
Into the Hollow (EIT #6)
And With Madness Comes the Light (EIT #6.5)
Come Alive (EIT #7)
Ashes to Ashes (EIT #8)
Dust to Dust (EIT #9)

Novels by Karina Halle

The Devil's Metal (Devils #1)
The Devil's Reprise (Devils #2)
Sins and Needles (The Artists Trilogy #1)
On Every Street (An Artists Trilogy Novella #0.5)
Shooting Scars (The Artists Trilogy #2)
Bold Tricks (The Artists Trilogy #3)
Donners of the Dead
Dirty Angels
Dirty Deeds
Dirty Promises
Love, in English
Love, in Spanish
Where Sea Meets Sky (from Atria Books)
Racing the Sun (from Atria Books)
Before the Dawn (from Atria Books)
Bright Midnight (from Atria Books)
The Pact
The Offer
The Play
Winter Wishes
The Lie
The Debt

Winter Wishes

A novella

By Karina Halle

METAL BLONDE BOOKS

\m/ Metal Blonde Books \m/

First edition published by
Metal Blonde Books December 2015

Cover design by Hang Le Designs

ISBN-13: 978-1523434107

Metal Blonde Books
P.O. Box 845
Point Roberts, WA
98281 USA

Manufactured in the USA
For more information visit:
http://authorkarinahalle.com/

PLEASE NOTE: Winter Wishes is NOT a standalone. It takes place after the last chapter of The Play but before the epilogue.

For my Anti-Heroes

CHAPTER ONE

Kayla

"Morning, love."

For a moment, I can't tell if I'm dreaming or not. Lachlan's thick Scottish brogue has this way of invading my dreams, blurring the line between fantasy and reality. But, hey, how many people can say the man of their dreams is the man of their life? Even when I wake up, I'm acutely aware of how lucky I am to be Lachlan McGregor's love.

I know. How cheesy. And thank god for that, because if I didn't have Lachlan by my side, in my bed, wherever I can have him, I would be losing my fucking mind.

It's been ten days since I threw caution to the wind and took the greatest risk of my life by leaving everything I ever knew behind in San Francisco, and came to

Edinburgh on somewhat of a whim, hoping to rekindle the love I never stopped dreaming about. It's been ten days of hot, passionate sex, long conversations and sloppy dog kisses. It's also been ten days of second-guessing my decision, biting my nails, and missing Steph, Nicola, and my brothers back at home. Not to mention the grief over my mother, which is ever-present and bone-deep. To say I've been torn in a million different directions is an understatement.

But Lachlan has been by my side every step of the way, so no matter which direction my thoughts and heart and soul have been leaning, his very being reminds me that I'm not alone in it. I honestly don't know what I'd do without him. I wouldn't be here, that's for sure.

I must sink briefly back into sleep again until I feel his lips press softly against my forehead.

"You can't sleep forever," he murmurs, his breath hot on my skin. "You'll want to get up before the snow melts."

Snow?

I open my eyes as he pulls away and peers down at me. His eyes look especially green in the morning light, crinkling at the corners as a hint of a smile tugs at his lips. Damn, those lips of his. He's so fucking handsome it's like walking around with a permanent colony of butterflies in my stomach.

"What are you talking about?" I ask softly, my voice still groggy with sleep.

He nods his head at the window just as Lionel jumps up on the bed and starts licking my face. I playfully shove him out of the way and sit up to look outside.

I gasp.

He wasn't kidding.

A thin layer of snow blankets the park across the street, frosting the grass and sticking to bare branches like icing sugar. "Oh my god," I say, unable to take my eyes away from the blinding white scene. "Does this normally happen?"

"Sometimes," Lachlan says. "It used to snow more often, but you know, bloody climate change and all that."

I look at him with wide, hopeful eyes. "Does this mean we'll have a white Christmas?"

He shrugs. "Maybe."

I tilt my head at him. "Oh, come on, you're supposed to be more excited than that. I've never had a white Christmas before. I used to ask Santa for one every year and obviously that never came true."

"Maybe you were a naughty girl."

I grin, hitting him on his rock-hard bicep. "You know I was."

He nods slowly, his eyes trailing over my mouth, neck, chest. Teasing. "Still are," he says, his voice dropping a register. "Very much so."

The hairs on my neck stand on end, my skin coming alive from just his gaze. As usual, it takes nothing more than a look from him to turn me on. He doesn't even have to be around to drive me crazy. I never thought I would become one of those girls that masturbate over their own boyfriend instead of a model or celebrity crush, but there's a first time for everything.

He leans down, eyes fluttering closed, and kisses the corner of my mouth before slowly sweeping his lips across my jaw. So warm, wet, and soft. I sink back into the pillow, his lips like the sweetest drug. He presses against me and I can feel his hard, stiff length through his jeans, and I instinctively press my hips up to meet his, craving him inside me. I'm wet within seconds and desperate for him to get closer.

"Why are you not always naked?" I practically whimper, sliding my hands underneath his white t-shirt and down the hard, smooth planes of his muscular back. I could touch that back of his for hours.

"Because I'm a stupid, stupid man," he whispers, sucking my neck into his mouth. The moan it elicits is loud but being noisy is something I refuse to be embarrassed about. Besides, he likes it. What man doesn't want to hear just what kind of pleasure they're giving to a woman?

"A stupid man with a great big dick," I tease him, reaching under and palming his erection.

"Perfect for the girl with the tight little cunt." His voice gets all low and growly over the last word and he licks down to my collarbone, bathing me in sparks.

Damn. The dirty mouth comes out to play.

I fumble for his jeans, undoing them as quickly as I can, while he pulls his shirt over his head. God, the sight of him above me, every hard-earned, rippled muscle, every beautiful, telling tattoo—it just never gets old.

He reaches back to yank off his jeans when Lionel springs forward, grabbing the hem with his teeth and pulling playfully.

"Glad you're trying to help, mate," Lachlan says to Lionel, laughing as the pit bull tugs them off. Lachlan shoots me an apologetic look before getting off the bed. "Don't worry, he's on his way out."

I know it's super silly, but I just can't fuck when there are dogs in the room. Lachlan assures me they don't know the difference, but I *know* they know. It's weird. I can be an exhibitionist in some ways but not in that one.

Lachlan pulls off the rest of his jeans and strides across the room, shooing Lionel out. He's commando as he often is and I have the world's best view of the world's best ass. All those years of rugby and now boxing have firmed that behind into a sculpted peach that I just want to sink my teeth and nails into. That, plus those broad shoulders and the sinewy muscles of his back, the dimples at his waist, his thick, impossibly strong quads—he's man overload. Sometimes I wish I was a guy just so I could fuck him from behind because what a hell of a view that would be.

He closes the door on Lionel then turns around, another perfect sight. He's holding his gorgeous dick in his hand and my eyes are torn between indulging in the beautiful, wanting part of his lips and his thick cock on display.

"You ready for me?" he asks, and the look on his face is practically smoldering.

Why does he even ask?

I smile, ever the coquette, then pull my camisole over my head. Last night we'd had sex before we fell asleep and I hadn't even bothered to put underwear back on, which was coming in handy right now.

Lachlan walks over and stops right beside the bed, his eyes burning down at me.

"Want to play this morning?" he asks gruffly, though his lips are quirking up into a wicked smile.

"Play?" I ask, mildly confused. "Or fuck?"

He reaches down and pulls open the bedside table drawer. "Both." He takes out the silky sleep mask that I got from the airplane ride over here. "Put this on."

I take it from him. Hmmm. Okay. So *this* is playing.

I slip it over my head, pulling it down over my eyes until the world goes almost black, only a faint glow of grey coming through from underneath the edge.

"Lie back," he tells me, and I shiver from the sound of his voice, so throaty, husky, and extra commanding in the dark.

I lie back and feel his hand slip under my head, pulling the pillow down so I'm more comfortable. Then I feel him step away from me, and hear the sound of him rummaging. The snap of a container opening.

"What are you doing?" I ask him, my pulse starting to dance.

"Something I've fantasized about," he says.

Fantasies? Yes, please.

"Let's have it," I tell him.

"Just relax. Don't move. Don't talk. I'm going to do some pretty messy things to you."

Oh, sweet Jesus.

"Starting with these fantastic tits of yours," he says, nearly growling. I hear his hands slap together and then he climbs on top of me, his strong, warm legs on either side of my waist.

I think I have an idea where this is going.

I suck in my breath, my body tensed and waiting for his next move.

His hands slide slickly down the middle of my chest and outward across each breast. The faint smell of mint sneaks in and I know he's rubbed me over with lube. Normally I don't need the stuff, but, well, you can't really take it up the ass without it.

Though at the moment, it's my tits that are getting all oiled up. He spreads it on as if he's rubbing it into my skin, giving me a massage, only it's not relaxing in the slightest. The slick press of his fingers ignite my nerves, the heat building with each stroke. His tongue teases at one of my nipples, already stiff and begging for it.

My moan gets caught in my throat and I writhe under him, reaching for the back of his neck to pull him closer.

"I said don't move," he commands, and I immediately drop my hand down to my side. Sheesh. Bossy.

He takes my nipple in his teeth and tugs. It's just the slightest bit painful, but more than that, it causes a shower of electricity to hum out from my limbs.

"Fuck," I say breathlessly.

He pauses. "I said don't talk. I'll stop what I'm doing right now if you do."

I can't tell he means business but being quiet has never been my strong suit. I press my lips together in exaggeration until I feel his mouth back on my nipples again, licking and sucking while I swell between my legs, so very desperate, so very unable to do anything about it.

This is torture. Beautiful, sweet torture.

With the mask on, with my nerves fighting against the silence, against my body's natural urge to move, to touch him, to writhe and beg, my world is burning, on fire, and I'll just be ashes in the end.

His head goes lower, licking down the center of my stomach until he gets between my legs. I know he's enjoying the torture, murmuring against me as he kisses down the V of my hipbones, then as he slides his long, wet tongue where my legs and pelvis meet. The skin there is so sensitive I nearly cry out as he gently laps at it, teasing up the sides, coming close to my clit and then backing away.

"Please," I can't help but moan. Suddenly he smacks the side of my thigh. Hard.

"This is your last warning," he says. God, his brogue, his gravely voice, he's beyond hot when he's domineering. He would be a pretty good Dom because he's so good at the pain and torture. Only it's not what he does to me but what he doesn't do. He has me wanting him so badly I can barely breathe.

Finally his tongue snakes along my clit and I suck in a sharp breath, trying to compose myself. I'm seconds from coming and he knows this. He works me fast, his tongue flicking rapidly and so hard as I swell beneath him, the pressure in my core building and building in hot hot heat.

Then he withdraws and I'm nearly left gasping for him.

The fucking tease.

"Easy now," he says gruffly. "You're doing so good love. I may just reward you."

He straddles me with his heavy thighs and I feel himself position the hard tip of his dick to me. With slow ease he pushes himself inside as I widen around him, my body needing him, craving him. In seconds he's in to the hilt, he's a part of me and I don't think I've ever felt so beautifully stretched.

"You feel so fucking good," he groans as he pulls himself out and thrusts in again, his rigid length dragging along all the right spots. "So good. So beautiful. You drive me mad, you know. All the time. All the fucking time."

I gasp as he drives in harder and then freezes up, thinking he may quit on me as punishment, but he lets it slide. He starts pumping into me faster, deeper, and it takes all of my resolve not to reach up for his firm ass and hold him inside me.

I can feel the sweat drip from his body onto mine and I'm surprised I'm not sizzling. He slips his hand down, making a fist over the base of his cock as it slides into me, and in his breathless, low voice, tells me how perfect I am, how much he loves me, how much he loves fucking me, how tight and sweet and wet I am. My mind is filled with his dirty words, my heart filled with his love and my cunt filled with every inch of his thick, hard-as-steel cock.

His fingers then slide over my clit, in rhythm with his merciless thrusts.

One.

Two.

The band of fire inside me crackles.

Snaps.

All bets are off.

I come, moaning loudly, calling out his name as starbursts form beneath the mask and my body explodes in a hot wash of nerves and champagne. I'm writhing, bucking, floating into pure bliss. Away, away, away.

Fuck.

This man.

"Not over yet love," he says, pulling out of me as I still pulse around him.

He slowly inches forward over me, still straddling as he works his way up, and I can feel his balls brush over the soft expanse of my abdomen until they stop just below my chest.

Ah, yes. This.

"Do I have permission to help you out?" I ask, clearing my throat.

"Permission granted," he says as he positions his cock, hot and wet, between my breasts and then cups them, pushing them into the middle. I don't have the biggest breasts in the world for this kind of thing but when I place my hands on top of his and really press them in, it works.

He slides his cock back and forth between them, the lube slick, and I revel in the primal sound of his grunts and groans above me as he works harder and harder. A few times he slips out, but I shoo his hands away so he can grab the headboard. I get a better grip on the sides of my breasts and really make him feel it.

"Oh, fuck. Fuck me." He groans. "Your tits. You're unbelievable, love."

Damn right I am.

His pumps become quicker and I know he's going to come any second. The way his breath hitches, the way his thighs tense up, the little sounds he probably doesn't know he makes. Desperate sounds. Needy sounds.

Sounds that tell me that I'm turning him on like nothing else in this world can.

I fucking live for those sounds.

And he comes. He comes with a hoarse cry and his cum shoots forward all over my neck and face, hot, wet, sticky. Personally I love it when he comes all over me, it's so dirty, so messy, so carnal. Like a fucking animal. I'm just grateful for the eye mask this time because I would have probably gone blind from the cum in my eye. I hear it's good for the skin, but I'm not too sure about vision.

He groans, moaning my name, breathing hard for a few moments before he reaches for the tissues beside the bed and delicately cleans me up.

I take off the mask, blinking at him and the flush on his face, the lazy slant to his eyes. So at peace. So gorgeous.

"Good morning," I tell him as he lies down beside me, holding me to him.

"Good morning," is his throaty, languid reply.

Together we lie there, lost in the sheets, in each other's arm, in the silence of nothing but our beating hearts.

I nearly fall asleep this way but he shakes me gently.

"Come on, let's take the dogs to the park," he says to me, getting off the bed. "Unless Emily was raised outside of California before she was a stray, she's probably never seen snow before. She's going to lose her shite over this."

"I'm going to lose my *shite*," I tell him, mimicking his accent. Though I'm reluctant to leave the warmth of the covers and that post-orgasm bliss is still fogging my mind, aside from never having had a white Christmas before, I've only seen snow a handful of times.

I get dressed quickly, pulling on fleece joggers, fuzzy socks, and a thick sweater (or "jumper," as Lachlan and everyone else in this country calls it). The dogs are going nuts. Lionel is running in circles around the drawing room, Emily is hiding under the coffee table and barking, and sweet, elderly Jo is sitting by the door, waiting for her leash, tail thumping against the floor.

We slip the muzzles on Jo and Lionel—though I was only away from the UK for about three months or so, I had been hoping they'd relax their dangerous breed ban, but no such luck—then put on our coats and head down the stairs and outside.

"Wow," I say as we stand on the stoop surveying the winter wonderland. My breath freezes in the air and floats away, the morning sun shooting through low clouds and lighting the snow in columns of pale gold. I can't think of a more beautiful place to be swathed in snowfall than Edinburgh. All the stone row houses look like they're made of gingerbread. Most are trimmed with Christmas lights and wreaths, and through some windows you can see giant trees in the drawing rooms done up in shiny tinsel.

"When I woke up this morning it was still coming down," he says, squinting up at the sky. "I was hoping that by the time I got back from boxing it would still be falling."

"This is beautiful," I tell him, and though I wish I could have seen the snow fall, I also know that Lachlan gets up at six in the morning and that's out of the question for me. Sometimes he goes boxing, sometimes he just takes the dogs for a long walk. He's doing phenomenally well in his effort to remain sober. Going to a psychiatrist, taking low dose anti-anxiety medication. Above all, extra exercise seems to keep his demons in check. As if playing rugby professionally wasn't enough, now he has to keep himself nearly exhausted. Not that I'm complaining though—his body is looking better than ever, something I never thought possible, and it's made him even more vigorous in the sack. We've got a lot of lost time to make up for.

He grabs my hand and gives it a squeeze. With the other he holds Emily's leash while I hold Jo and Lionel, the muzzle twins. I guess they're less scary when I hold them, the tiny Asian girl, versus Lachlan and his big, badass, tattooed self.

Also there's the fact that Emily is skittish around anyone except for him. Although at this moment, she's especially freaked out, gingerly sniffing the snow, her eyes wide, hair standing on end.

We carefully make our way down the steps and cross the street toward the park. I marvel at the way the snow shimmers in the light, the chill in the air that seems to drive out all the city smog. I lean into Lachlan's solid mass, feeling absolutely cozy. Happy. Whatever uncertainty I had about coming here, no matter how brief it had been, seems to have been wiped clean.

Still, there's no ignoring the fact that I have yet to find a job, not to mention that next week I'll be spending Christmas up north with his family at his grandfather's house outside of Aberdeen. I'm trying not to let Lachlan know how much it's freaking me out. I know I've already met his adopted parents, Jessica and Donald, but that was back before we split up, before my mother died, before our lives went to shit. I haven't seen them since I've been back—Lachlan's been pretty busy with rugby as it is—and I'm on edge about meeting his grandfather, George. From what I've heard, he's a bit of a cantankerous grouch, and that's coming from Lachlan who rarely says anything bad about anyone.

While we check to see if the park is clear before we let the dogs off the leashes, Lionel and Jo fluffing up the snow while Emily still seems utterly bewildered, I ask him, "Do you think there will be snow up in Aberdeen?"

He opens his mouth to say something. I'm guessing he wants to say "maybe." But he just smiles, nodding once, and then says, "Yes, I do." He pulls me close to him, wrapping his strong arms around my waist, and studies my face. "Are you worried?"

"About the snow?"

He squints at me. "About Christmas. About being around my family, staying there, when you haven't been around them often."

How this man manages to read me so well, I don't know.

I rub my lips together, wishing I'd brought some ChapStick with me. "Yeah, a little. I'll be fine. I'm more worried about getting them all the right Christmas presents, to be honest." I sigh and lean my head against his chest. "And then I start thinking about having enough money to buy them, then I start thinking about how badly I want this writing job, then I think about what happens if I don't get it. What am I going to do with myself? And then I wish I could just…" I trail off, swallowing hard. "I wish I could talk to my mother about this, just for a second, you know?"

He exhales heavily and kisses the top of my head. "Kayla, love," he says gently. "I know none of this is going to be easy for you, and what you can give to me, I'll happily take. But my family should be the least of your worries. Really. They don't need anything for Christmas and you know they already love you."

"I've never met your grandpa," I mumble into him. "You said he was grumpy."

"Aye," he says with a bit of a laugh. "You know I don't sugarcoat things. But if I can handle him, you can handle him. Besides, he's gotten a bit better with age."

"I thought you said he'd gotten worse with age."

"I guess it depends on the Christmas," he says, sounding unsure now. "To be honest with you, he's never been all that accepting of me to begin with. Viewed me as the black sheep of the family. Even now, though I should be grateful that he considers me family at all."

I look up at him. He's staring off into the distance, frowning, and I know he's being pulled into a darker place. "Of course you're family. He's had, what, almost twenty years to get used to you. You're a McGregor. You're family."

He nods. "Aye," he says absently. "But he's always treated me different from the way he treats Brigs, which is to be expected. I just don't know if he knows anything about, well, my current condition. Jessica and Donald may not have mentioned my…problem."

What he's meaning to say is that he's an alcoholic. I know admitting it is the supposed first step, but it still takes a lot for Lachlan to say it out loud sometimes. I don't push it. He's doing so well as it is, and he knows exactly what his problem is.

But really, something like the holidays is just the kind of thing to fuck life all up. All this time I've been fretting about my own problems, but suddenly it's clear that this isn't any easier on him. I had no idea about Lachlan and his grandfather's relationship.

"Does he like to drink?" I ask him.

"A bit much, in my opinion, for whatever that's worth. I know when I go home or out with Brigs, they don't drink in front of me. Which I appreciate. I don't know how that will go down with George. He's a stubborn shit. But I'll deal with it."

I squeeze his arm, gazing up at him imploringly. "And I'll help you deal."

He smiles softly at me, the snow lighting up his face. "Promise?"

"Promise."

We stand there for a few more minutes in that winter wonderland, watching Lionel frolic in the snow, Jo rolling around on her back making doggie snow angels, and Emily just staring at this cold new world, thoroughly unimpressed like a regular old Scrooge.

Oh well, you can't win them all.

CHAPTER TWO

Lachlan

"So when are you going to ask her to marry you?"

Brigs' question is so out of the blue that it takes everything not to spit out my coffee. Instead, I choke on it.

"What?" I manage to say, coughing into my arm, my eyes watering. "Bloody hell, Brigs."

He gives me a faint smile, his ice blue eyes looking positively devilish. He shrugs with one shoulder, observing me with amusement. "I think it's a fair question."

I swallow the rest of my coffee and lean back in my chair, shaking my head. "Is that why you asked me out for coffee? Did your mom put you up to this?"

His features slacken, unimpressed. "No. Not at all." I know he wants to add that she's my mother too, regardless if I'm adopted, but he lets it slide this time. "But I can't help noticing that Kayla moved all the way to Scotland for you. This isn't some casual fling."

"This never was casual," I say, giving him a measured look. "You know that."

He nods, knowing all too well what Kayla and I have been through already, and taps his fingers along the edge of the wooden table, looking out the window. The temperature has been cold enough so the dusting of snow from the other night hasn't melted, and though the city streets have turned to mush, there's something almost fairytale-like about Edinburgh at the moment. I make a note to take Kayla to Princes Street later to really soak up the atmosphere.

Even though I meet with Brigs once every week or so, there was something in his voice when he called this morning which made me think he had something on his mind. And the way he's fidgeting when he normally remains so calm only adds to my suspicion.

"So why are we really here today?" I ask him carefully. "Not that I mind, I can just tell that something is on your mind and it isn't me and Kayla."

Also, to be honest, I'm happy for a subject change. The way I feel about Kayla is so intense, and so personal, it's almost overpowering at times. I still can't believe that she's here, that she came back to me. For me. For herself. The last thing I want to do is jinx it all by wondering about marriage.

Not that the thought hasn't crossed my mind.

It's been crossing it a lot, actually. In fact, every time I feel myself being pulled into the shadows, every time my hands shake because of the need to drink, to escape, I think about her. I think about just that. I think about the person I need to be for her, forever.

The thought only calms me. It doesn't scare me.

But it could scare her. So I keep it to myself. And even though Brigs is one of the closest people to me, I don't want to share that with him just yet.

The drumming of his fingers stops. "Well," he says slowly, "you're right about that." He clears his throat and gives me a hopeful look. "I've been offered a teaching position."

He says it so casually that I hesitate before saying, "Really?"

"It's in London. King's College."

I shake my head in disbelief. Brigs lost his job here at the university when his wife and child died in a car accident a few years ago. He'd found a new position in the fall, but unfortunately due to budget cuts, they let him go after a month or so, which was total rubbish. But this, Kings College, is something he's been wanting for a long time.

"That's brilliant," I exclaim, leaning over and slapping him on the arm. I know I'm grinning like a fool, hoping he'll finally give in and smile. Not that I'm one to talk, but getting a genuine smile out of Brigs these days isn't an easy task. "In film?"

He adjusts the scarf around his neck. "Yes. Professor of film studies. They want me for the undergraduate film theory curriculum."

"They want you? You mean, they have you."

"I haven't accepted yet."

I frown. "Why not?"

He looks away and shrugs. "It's in London."

"And? You like London."

"I don't," he says quickly. "And you're here."

"Brigs," I say slowly. "I'm fine. Really. I appreciate the sentiment, but for God's sake, this is something you've been waiting for. Working for. Anyway, you're a train ride away from Edinburgh. Have you told Jessica and Donald?"

He shakes his head and takes a tepid sip of his coffee. "No. I will. I just wanted to tell you first. I think I need some convincing."

I scratch at my beard. "Well, mate, I don't know how to convince you. All I know is that this is exactly what you've wanted. What you've needed."

And that's the truth. I don't need to mention that getting out of Edinburgh will probably do him a world of good. The city has too many memories for him. Every time I feel sorry for myself and my own struggles—my addictions, my abandonment issues—I think about Brigs and how he lost absolutely everything. To see him bounce back from it is astounding. The fact that his future is finally opening up to him after all that is nothing short of a miracle.

"Aye," he says softly. "I do think I need this."

"So tell them that you accept."

He studies me for a moment. There's a flash of something in his eyes, worry maybe, but I can't tell if it's for me or for himself.

"When would you start?" I ask.

"Not until next year. Autumn. But I would move there at the end of the semester, before summer. There's a lot to do before classes start, and I'm not going into this opportunity unprepared."

"This is going to be really good for you, you know this. Professor McGregor again."

Finally a smile breaks across his face, wide and always disarming. "Yes, well I'll miss Scotland, that's for sure. But change…I'm ready for it. I dare think it's ready for me."

Though we aren't related by blood, we're alike in so many ways. Like me, Brigs doesn't like to dwell on things for too long, especially anything that requires you to dig deep. He brings up rugby, an easy subject for both of us to talk about.

But as he goes on, making fun of some of my plays, because that's what he does, I can't help but drift back to what Kayla had said yesterday about Christmas. How hard it's going to be on her. It won't be any easier for Brigs. And with all the alcohol around the holidays, the stress, plus having to deal with George, who, if I'm being honest here, can be a racist, judgemental prick at times, it looks like it's shaping up to be one hell of a Christmas.

Just the thought of it all brings back the demons, slithering up through my veins like old friends. I order another coffee to combat it (caffeine has become my best friend in this battle), say goodbye to Brigs, and then head back to the flat and Kayla.

"How was Brigs?" she asks me as I come in the door and kick off my boots. Lionel jumps up at me, tongue lolling out of his wide mouth, before running back to the couch to cuddle with Jo.

I take off my beanie and jacket, hanging them up. "He's great, actually."

I tell her the news about his job in London.

"Oh my god," she says, clapping her hands together and making a little squeeing sound that I find so bloody adorable. "That's so exciting! He must be so happy! What's he like when he's happy?"

I chuckle and head into the kitchen to put on the kettle. "Well, he's a bit on the fence about it. I don't know why, really. He says he's not a fan of London, which is odd because he used to love going there."

"Maybe he's just afraid of the change," she says, leaning against the doorway, watching me. I glance at her while I fill the kettle. Her brows are knit together, thinking. "You know, in some ways it was really hard for me to come here. Not just in the whole moving countries thing, but…leaving San Francisco was like leaving her." She swallows hard and I can practically see the grief washing over her. "I felt like the city was my last tie to her. But…it was time. I had to move on. I couldn't stay there." She looks up at me, tears in her eyes. "I couldn't stand another minute without you."

Jesus. There she goes, my beautiful world, breaking my heart into pieces.

I put the kettle down and stride over to her, scooping her up into my arms. She's so fragile lately, like the finest crystal.

"Hey," I whisper into her hair, holding her tight. "I've got you."

She whimpers into me, breathing hard. "I just wish it would end. I feel so torn up inside. All the time. Every minute. I love you so much, Lachlan, I really do. And it makes me so fucking happy. But then I remember what I've lost, how much I miss my mother, and I just don't know how to feel anymore. My heart has schizophrenia."

"I think that's normal," I tell her gently. "And I wish it could just get easier right away, but these things take time. You're going to feel great and then you're going to backslide. But no matter what, I don't want you to feel guilty for your happiness. That's all your mother ever wanted for you. You need to own that."

She sighs. "I know. I know."

"Tell you what," I say, pulling back and tipping her chin up with my fingers. Even with tears streaming down her face, she's unbearably beautiful. "Tonight I'm going to take you to the Christmas fair on Princes Street. We're going to eat a load of rubbish and go on all the rides until we're sick. Sound good?"

Finally I see that smile. "That sounds both amazing and terrible. I'm down."

"Good," I say, brushing my thumbs over her cheeks and clearing away the tears. I kiss her softly on her lips until she relaxes into me.

I know I've made her feel safe again, if only for a short while.

***

The Edinburgh Christmas market is one of the most beautiful holiday markets in the world. Kayla and I had been by a few times during the day, but we were usually on our way to and from somewhere. At night it's a completely different experience.

Picture this: the long straight line of Princes Street completely lit up in white, gold, green, and red. The towering shops with their twinkling and elaborate Christmas displays are on one side, while the Princes Street Gardens on the other are filled with market stalls, glittering rides such as the Christmas tree slide, the double carousel, the Star Flyer, the Big Wheel, and even Santa's train. People are everywhere, bundled up, laughing—kids are running around, and it all smells of caramel corn, mulled wine, and pine needles. Christmas songs and carollers in all directions bring in the surround sound.

It's pure Christmas bliss, if you're into that kind of thing, and I think it's exactly what Kayla needs to get into the spirit, to put a smile on her face.

"Oh my god," Kayla says as we turn the corner and the whole sparkling world lights up before us. She's so wide-eyed, like a little kid, that I can't help but grin at her, squeezing her tight to me. "This looks so amazing!"

"I thought it might cheer you up," I tell her. "It's impossible to be in a bad mood here."

"Yeah," she says, looking around her at the crowds wandering to and fro. "Even though people are like my least favorite thing, at least here everyone looks happy."

I'm not big on crowds or people either—probably one of the many reasons why the two of us work so well together—but here it just adds to the flavor of things. It's amazing what you're willing to forgive at this time of year.

Kayla wants to go on the Big Wheel, so we head on down to it.

"I thought you were afraid of heights," I say, craning my neck back to look at the giant Ferris wheel with the enclosed pods. Shadows of people lean against them, staring at what must be an astounding view.

"I am," she admits. "But I think this whole embracing your fears thing is rubbing off on me."

But when we get near the line we hear the wait is at least an hour. So we stroll over to the market stalls instead. We both get cups of steaming hot mulled wine. I get the non-alcoholic version and so does Kayla. I've told her a few times that just because I don't drink anymore doesn't mean she has to, but she always dismisses it. Her support in just the most subtle of ways undoes me sometimes.

"Hey, help me pick out something for your family," she says, taking my hand and pulling me toward some of the vendors.

I look over everything, most things geared toward Christmas, tapping my fingers against my lips. "Jessica and Donald are both easy and hard to shop for," I tell her. "I know that doesn't bloody help much, but it's true. They have everything they could want, but what they always love is something personal. Something that made you think of them, that you could see in their house."

"That helps," she says, looking at me hopefully. "Want to go in on a present with me?"

I smile at her. "Of course I do. But you're picking it out."

She gives me an exaggerated pout before turning her attention back to the rows of goods. "Fine. But if you think they'll hate it, you have to tell me."

"Deal."

It's funny watching Kayla as she tries to find just the right gift. She goes from stall to stall, asking the vendors questions, examining every item like she's an appraiser at an auction. Finally she settles on a plastic box of delicate glass Christmas ornaments that look about a hundred years old.

"They're vintage," she tells me, reading the tag. "Jessica has such an eye for design, especially antiques. At least that's what I could tell from their house." She hands it to me. "Look close at the pattern. There are miniature Edinburgh landmarks inside the glass, done up like frost."

I peer at it and spot Edinburgh Castle in one, the cathedral in another, blending seamlessly inside the glass balls like a miniature, snow-covered world. It's very beautiful and I think Jessica would think it's absolutely brilliant. Donald would just be happy with whatever makes his wife happy.

"Done," I say, fishing out some notes and handing it over to the vendor who takes it happily.

"Now on to Brigs," she says, grasping the bag to her chest.

"He's easy," I tell her. "Highball glasses for his Scotch. He collects them."

She raises her eyebrow. "That's a little too easy. Let me guess, you've been giving him that gift for years now."

I shrug. "We're both pretty low maintenance in the gift department. And that's a hint from me to you. Meaning, don't get me anything."

"Oh, I won't," she says, even though I know she will. Which reminds me, I've got to get her a gift. I've been stewing over it all week, and I still can't come up with anything. There's really nothing on the planet that could possibly express what she means to me.

"Brigs teaches film, right?" she asks as we get ourselves hot roasted chestnuts. "I mean, even though he teaches it, he's obviously a film buff."

I nod. "Aye," I say, before inhaling the smell of the chestnuts. That always solidifies Christmas for me. Even when I was a young lad and didn't have a proper Christmas, my birth mother always bought some for me every December. It's one of the few good memories I have from growing up. In some ways, those rarities made it harder in the coming years.

"So," she says as we walk by a stall where a caricature artist is presently sketching a squirming little girl. "We could get one of this guy's prints." She nods at the art lining the wall of the tent, some of random people, others celebrities, from Audrey Hepburn to Kanye West. "Or," she goes on, "you have a picture of him on your phone, right? We could get a caricature of him drawn as whatever film dude he likes."

"Film dude?" I repeat, biting my lip to keep from laughing.

She rolls her eyes, slapping my arm. "You know what I mean."

I sigh, folding my arms across my chest and peering at the range of drawings. It would be utterly ridiculous to get Brigs something like this, but at the same time, I think he's the type to appreciate it for just how ridiculous it is. Maybe Kayla is right. The same old thing does get boring after a while, and it's always the thought that counts.

"Well, he's always been a big Buster Keaton fan," I tell her. "See if you can make that happen." I bring out my phone, flipping to a photo of Brigs and me together. We're both smiling, and he has his blindingly white, straight teeth on show. It's going to be real easy for the artist to make fun of that.

She snatches the phone out of my hand, peers at it closely, and then waits until the artist is done drawing the little girl before she explains what we want.

The man shrugs, as if he draws Brigs as Buster Keaton every day, and we agree on a price before he starts working.

"You know what I think Brigs needs?" Kayla says to me as the man draws, working a lot quicker than I thought he would. "A dog. You should convince him to adopt one of your shelter dogs."

I give her a wry smile, shoving my hands into my pockets. "Believe me, I've tried. After he lost Miranda and Hamish, I thought a dog could help him overcome the grief. But he hasn't been interested. Too wrapped up in his own world, which I get. And he loves dogs too—he always talks about Lionel and how one day he'll adopt. But I don't push it. I think dogs come to you when you need them just as much as when they need you."

"Kind of like you and Emily," she says.

"Like you *and* Emily," I correct her. "Not that you're a dog."

She raises her brow. "I'm a bitch sometimes."

I give her a dry look. "You both came to me when I needed you the most. It just took a while to realize it."

She grins at me. "Well, it was really only a week before you got a clue."

"Now that I know what I was missing, anything more than a second is an eternity."

It doesn't take long for the man to stop drawing, holding out the paper and admiring it with a curt nod of his head, like someone who has just painted a masterpiece.

He holds it out for us, and I have to hold back a laugh. In a way, it is a masterpiece. The guy has some talent...and a lot of that talent went toward making Brigs look as ridiculous as possible. He's got Buster Keaton's hat and the requisite bags under the eyes, but he's smiling—rare for both Keaton and Brigs—and his teeth take up half of his face.

Of course, Kayla being Kayla, doesn't hold back at all. She laughs—loudly—and points, shaking her finger at it.

"Oh my god!" she exclaims, clamping a hand over her mouth. "Look at Brigs! He looks fucking crazy. He's half Buster Keaton, half Mr. Ed." She looks at me, smiling big, a devious gleam in her eyes. "He's going to *hate* it. It's great."

The artist frowns at her, so I quickly pay him for it, telling him he did a great job. That doesn't stop him from glaring at Kayla as he slowly rolls up the portrait and slides a rubber band on it, smacking it on with a loud *snap*.

With the Christmas shopping all done, there really isn't much else to do but wander. A group of guys walk past, clenching beers in their gloves, and something inside me tightens. Darkens. Not quite like a flame going out, but like a silent, black fire spreading inside me.

I don't realize I'm clenching Kayla's hand—and my jaw—until she says, "What's wrong?"

My throat feels too thick to speak. My body is burning with oily flames and need, this horrible, unrelenting, unwanted need. Just from the simple sight of a few beers. If I weren't so busy being torn by simultaneous self-loathing and fear, I'd revel in the amazement. How I can go from normal and content in one minute to having my soul scream in the next is something I'll never understand and never get over.

Being an addict is a lot like grief. It permeates every essence of who you are.

I shake my head. "I'm okay," I manage to say, my voice gruff. "Let's just go home."

She nods, frowning. "Okay."

But as we head toward the street, she pulls me to a stop at one of the last stalls. Before I have a chance to ask her what she's doing, she's grabbing handfuls of tinsel in silver, red and green, a string of lights, plus a few cheap ornaments and a wiry gold star tree topper.

I have to admit, I'm grateful for the distraction, even though it's leaving me confused.

"But we don't have a tree," I tell her as she quickly pays for it all. I grab the bags from the merchant and we head on our way, cutting up Hanover Street.

"Don't worry about that," she says.

Once we're inside, the dogs run over to us, tails wagging, tongues hanging out, just happy to have us home. The flat itself seems to exhale with relief at our presence, or maybe it's just me.

"I better take them out," I tell her, grabbing the leashes.

"Before you do, do you mind putting on a fire?" she asks. "I want to make things all cozy for when you get back. In fact, take them for a longer than normal walk."

I pause. "What's going on?"

"Nothing," she says, though her tone suggests otherwise.

I observe her for a moment, loving how her lip quirks up just so when she's plotting something special. And with her, special usually means sexual. I have no complaints about that.

Though I never used the marble fireplace in the drawing room, since she's moved in we've had the fire going on chilly days. There's a small stack of wood left which I once kept primarily for ornamental reasons, so I throw in the remainder with some kindling and light a match.

When I'm satisfied the fire will stay strong, I get the whimpering pups and head back outside, throwing a glance at Kayla over my shoulder. She's nearly trembling with energy, her cheeks flushed. She's definitely got something planned.

I take my time walking the dogs, heading around the park and then down toward the Leith waterway. The stars above peek through fast moving white clouds, aglow from the city lights, and even though everything is merry and loud down on Princes Street, over here it's so quiet, like the neighborhood is holding its breath. Rows and rows of stone houses sit silently, lit in a range of Christmas lights. Some flats have displays out front in their tiny patch of a yard, maybe a Santa statue or a plastic snowman. Other places just have a wreath, a string of amber lights. As night falls deeper, so does the cold, and what remains of the snow crunches under my boots.

I'm glad Kayla asked me to go on a long walk. In fact, that's always been what's helped when I feel like I'm losing the battle against myself. Long walks. And sex. And I have a feeling she knows exactly what she's doing tonight.

And that's yet another reason why I'm so madly in love with her. It's not just about a connection—that tightened wire of energy that binds you to someone else. It's about what happens at either end of that wire. You're not just connected to that person, you *are* that person. Kayla knows me, all of me, and embraces every lost, crooked, damaged part.

I never have to say anything with her. She's inside me—she knows. And she loves me despite all that. In a world where magic isn't supposed to exist, I'm sometimes dumbfounded by love, because how can that be anything else but mystical, magical? Love bends reality to our will.

Emily gives a little bark beside me, snapping me out of my thoughts. I reach down and scoop her up in my arms. She gets colder easier than the other dogs and isn't afraid to let you know. Though I've never been a fan of dressing up dogs, perhaps a tiny Christmas sweater is in order for the grouchy old maid.

When I've been gone for about a half hour or so, I head back to the flat, nearly slipping on the ice outside before heading up the staircase to our level.

I pause outside the door, listening. I can hear Christmas music, some jazzy version, coming from inside.

"I'm back," I call out, stepping inside the foyer. I'm immediately hit with the warm smell of hot chocolate. The door to the dining room is open, but the one to the drawing room is closed. The dogs rush forward to the side table against the wall where a steaming mug of cocoa is resting. I deftly unleash them then pick up a note beside the mug.

Come by the fireplace and come alone. Bring the hot chocolate.

"Come alone," I read out loud. I raise my brow and look down at the dogs. "Sorry, guys. Those are my orders."

I pick up the mug and take a sip—it's thick, more like melted chocolate than hot chocolate, but it still tastes delicious—then put my hand on the doorknob to the drawing room, slowly turning it and pushing the door open.

Naturally the dogs rush toward me, but I push them back with my leg and step in, closing the door behind me.

The room is dark except for the fireplace, bathing the room in flickering light. It takes me a moment for my eyes to adjust, and I don't see Kayla anywhere until I realize I'm staring right at her silhouette by the window.

"Kayla?"

I take a few steps toward her and then stop. She's posed with her hands on her hips, but she's not moving at all. She's nothing but shadows and form, and I can't see her face.

"Go to the outlet by the far wall and plug in the socket," she says, her voice throaty.

"Okay," I say uncertainly. Now I have absolutely no idea what the hell is going on, but I do as she says.

There's a spark and then a glow beside me. I turn, and my mouth nearly drops on the floor as Kayla stands there, absolutely fucking naked, with Christmas tree lights wrapped around her, from her ankles to her neck.

"What the fuck," I say breathlessly, straightening up and running a hand over my jaw. "What are you doing, you crazy girl?"

She gives me a pointed look which is hard to take seriously when she's a naked Christmas tree. "I'm distracting you with Christmas cheer, that's what I'm doing. Now, decorate me." She nods at the box of tinsel and ornaments beside her.

I can only stare at her.

"I said, decorate me," she says. "I'm your Christmas tree. Do me justice."

Now this…this is something new. And even though I want to stand there, staring at her and scratching my head, I can see the faint flash of unease in her eyes, the idea that I may laugh at her, that she'll become embarrassed. I love it when Kayla gets all red in the cheeks over something but not when she's bare and vulnerable and out on a limb.

Literally, too. Because I'm going to have to pretend she's a bloody tree.

"Yes, m'am." I reach down for a long string of silver tinsel and look up her naked, glowing body. "Where do I start?"

"Anywhere you want," she says.

So I start down at her ankles. I wind the tinsel around the wire of the lights to keep it in place, then I bring it around and around and up her calves, her thighs.

I pause between her legs and slide my fingers up the soft skin of her inner thighs. "Here?" I ask, my voice already husky with lust. I can't ignore the fact that I have one hell of a hard-on straining against my jeans, something that will have to be dealt with in a major way before the night is over.

"Mmm," she says and I drag my fingers between her pussy, lightly skirting over clit. I'm not even sure if I want to continue, especially when she moans so loudly and her legs start to shake.

"Don't stop now," she whispers and I press one finger, then two into her, so tight and wet, it's intoxicating. She squeezes around my finger and it's like a hot vice on my balls, my cock, my chest. All the air leaves my lungs.

"No," she says, voice low and straining. "Don't stop decorating. It can't be over yet."

"Oh, you're no fun. I've never made a Christmas tree come before."

"You will, believe me," she says.

Reluctantly I withdraw my fingers and drag her wetness over her stomach, having a bit of fun as I press the tinsel into her. "Well, if you're giving me free rein here," I say. "I mean, the tinsel doesn't want to stay on you on its own."

She grins at me, her face lit by her own lights, looking both ridiculous and ridiculously sexy. "That's what the hot chocolate is for. I made it extra *thick* for this purpose. Or, you know, your own contribution, though let's save that for later, shall we?"

I look behind me at the mug of hot chocolate and pick it up. It was already too thick and rich before and now that it's cooled down, it resembles melted chocolatey mud.

Without hesitation I dip my fingers into the mug, still warm, and start painting her body with it. I make my way up her soft stomach, alternating between painting it on and licking it right off, then smearing it up over her breasts, taking extra time over the hardened pebbles of her nipples.

She gasps, looking shaky again, so I bring up the tinsel, pressing it in until it sticks. I slather on more chocolate – all over her delicate throat, her thin collarbones, her shoulders, her arms, moving around to her spine, the small of her back, her perky little arse. I get more tinsel, gold now and green, and continue to drape it around her, over and over again.

I'm turned on as hell. My cock strains against my fly, nearly fighting its way out. I'm not sure how much longer I can last, hold it together. The thing is, this may be the strangest way anyone has ever tried to cheer me up or distract me but I'm sure as hell grateful I've got a mastermind like Kayla by my side.

"Now the ornaments," she says, adjusting her weight from foot to foot. I know she's getting tired of standing so I make it quick.

Luckily, the only ornaments in the box are of the soft felt variety. Nothing made of glass or metal that might shatter or hurt us the moment I decide to throw her to the ground. Because, let's face it, that's exactly what's going to happen.

I only manage to get on a few ornaments. Hanging two from her ears, a few from her fingers, when I growl, "Okay, I've had enough. I want you on the floor, on your knees, now."

"Not yet," she says, smiling like the she-devil she is. "You need to put on the star."

Oh for Christ's sake. I look down into the box and see the wiry star topper. I grab it, stretch out the gold wires so that it might balance on top of her head, then place it up there. Her crown.

I step back and admire her.

"How do I look?" she asks, her metallic and chocolate body lit up by the strings of lights.

She looks like a sexy alien queen, that's what. Someone from the weird sci-fi porn movies Brigs used to smuggle into the house when I was a teenager.

"You look like an angel," I tell her, hoping that sounds better. "All lit up like Christmas tree. From another planet. Actually you might be the strangest thing I've ever seen."

"But still hot enough to fuck, right?"

I can only growl in response. I stride over to her, feeling nothing inside me but hot blood and pulsing veins and the deep, deep need to ruin her. I created this gorgeous creature and now I'm going to defile her, revel in my power as creator.

And even deeper than that, I feel nothing but love for this woman who holds me in such regard, who always wants to help, even when I can't help myself.

I grab her by the waist and force her down to her knees while being careful she's not about to crunch any Christmas lights. Then I spin around her as she gets on all fours and I push the tinsel away from her arse. I knead her cheeks with my hands, sliding along the chocolate, spreading them and bringing them back together.

Then with one hand around her small, tinsel-covered waist, I unzip my jeans and bring out my cock, hot and pulsing in my hand. I know she's wet, I can practically smell her, and I press the purple head of my dick into her slickness, pushing in with a tight but easy thrust.

I groan, taking a moment to let the silky, hot feel of her envelope me.

Nothing on earth feels as good as this.

As her.

My Kayla.

My glowing queen.

Mine.

Then, after a long, teasing pause – in and out – I let loose.

The carnal, animalistic side of me takes over.

The side we both love.

I leave claw marks down her back, on her ass, on her thighs.

I spank her.

Defile her.

Call her the dirtiest names.

I pound her so hard that her head bobs from the impact, that the lights shimmer and shake and I feel like I'm fucking a bloody supernova.

It gets messy – hot chocolate and silver tinsel everywhere. It gets hot.

It gets harder, deeper, stronger.

I fuck her like I'll never see her again, have her again. I fuck her like I'm trying to leave a part of me inside her, one she'll never lose, no matter how hard she might try.

I fuck her until I'm coming hot and loud, the lights in my eyes, my cum shooting inside her, pumping out every last bit of me and she calls out my name and I call out hers.

We come together, as one, always one.

And when I have nothing left to give, I kiss up the mess of her back, her neck, her cheek as she turns her head and offers it to me. We're both breathing hard.

We're both such a mess.

And so bloody meant for each other.

CHAPTER THREE

Kayla

I wake up covered in tinsel.

Like, I know I'm totally naked, but I still resemble the tin man thanks to fragments of the stuff sticking to every inch of me. Shine a spotlight on me, spin me around, and I'm a veritable disco ball.

Jesus. Who knew Christmas could get so kinky? Though I suppose it was my idea for him to decorate me like a Christmas tree.

And my idea had worked, too. I could tell when he came home yesterday from meeting Brigs that he was having a tough go. It totally didn't help that bringing up Brigs led me into my own downward spiral of sorrow, sadness, and shame. I know I'm adding extra weight on Lachlan when I really don't want to. I want to be strong, I want to handle everything by myself. I want to make my mother proud, to fight through the grief on my own.

But fuck, it's hard. Lachlan's been so patient even though he's battling his own problems.

So I decided that maybe I needed to distract him more. Hell, let's be honest here, this is about distracting myself, too. If I'm not grieving my mother and fretting over my move here, I'm worrying about Lachlan or the job I badly want to get (which I should hear about any day now). And while our sex life doesn't need any improvement, the more we do it, the clearer our heads and hearts get. At least it seems to do that for me.

"Baby?" I call out, easing myself up in bed.

"Yup," I hear him say from the other room, and I sigh in relief. He pops his head into the bedroom, cup of coffee in hand, and eyes me, biting his lip with a smile.

"We made quite a mess," he says, coming forward and handing me the cup of coffee. "Here, I just poured it. I'll make myself another."

Before I can protest, he's leaving the room. I take a sip of the coffee then smile down at my silver self. I don't even have the decency to cover myself up. I'd walk around naked all the time if I could.

When he comes in with another cup for himself, I ask him, "Did you already go boxing?"

"Actually, no," he says, sitting on the corner of the bed. "Was feeling too lazy. Slept in for a bit and took the dogs for a walk. Was planning on going later. Did you want to come?"

I've never seen Lachlan box. I've been to rugby practices twice now since coming back, but he usually goes to boxing so early that I've never had the opportunity, even though he's invited me more than a few times.

"I'd love to," I tell him. "Do I get to fight you?"

He grins. It lights up his whole face, making him look boyish. "If you want. Or you can just watch, though I'm not sure how entertaining it will be for you. It's basically me sparring with Jake, my trainer, or taking it out on the bag." His eyes skirt over my body. "Did you want some help in getting that all off?"

"I wouldn't mind getting a good scrub down," I admit, straightening my leg and running my toe down the side of his thigh, an attempt at seduction. "Turns out cum and chocolate and tinsel create some kind of super paste."

"Who would have thought?"

We both finish our coffees in record time and end up in the shower together. I can hear Emily pawing at the door, something she does whenever the both of us are in here.

"You know," he says as he slides the shower puff down my arms, brow furrowed in concentration. "If you don't get the newspaper job…" I stiffen and he pauses, looking me in the eye. "I said 'if.' If you don't, you know you always have a job at Ruff Love."

I sigh, closing my eyes. Ever since I came back to Edinburgh, hoping to find a job, Lachlan has been offering me a position at his animal shelter. And I know, I know it's stupid that I don't just accept it. I guess it's just my stubborn pride that keeps winning out. I don't want to feel like I owe him anything, and even though the position would be legitimate, it's a bit weird to have your boyfriend paying your salary.

"I know you don't want to," he says softly, "but Amara needs the help. We're taking in more dogs all the time and we could make such a bigger difference if we had two of you on board. You wouldn't just be doing admin work, you'd be doing so much more and I know you'd be so good at it." He pauses, licking his lips as the water runs down his face. "It doesn't have to be the only job you do. And I'm not offering it to you because I'm in love with you. I'm offering it because I think it would make you happy."

It's funny. When I first visited the shelter, I thought there was no way that I could work there. Seeing all those sweet, abandoned dogs day in and day out, knowing that some of them would have to be put down in the end, that they would never find their forever homes, was heartbreaking. But after I went back a few times and really got to know Amara, the girl that runs it for Lachlan, I saw the hope in it all. The difference Lachlan's love, his organization, was making.

"I'll think about it," I tell him, as I always tell him. "I just really want to make it on my own, you know?"

"I know."

The only problem is, I'm trying to make it here by getting into the writing business. I built up a pretty good portfolio back in San Francisco. And I know the jobs aren't easy to come by, especially when I'm not a resident here, and if anything I'll end up freelancing. But if I could just get this job writing for the free daily newspaper, 24 Hours, it would not only provide me with something steady and (hopefully) permanent, but I'd feel like I accomplished something. Quitting my job at the Bay Area Weekly was one of the hardest things I ever had to do, though it had to be done. I just don't want to regress backward.

After I'm sparkling clean without an ounce of cum or tinsel on me, we get dressed and pile into Lachlan's Range Rover, heading to his gym.

I've seen a lot of boxing movies so I thought I knew what to expect. You know, a seedy, dark warehouse-type setting with lots of greasy, angry guys wearing hoodies and punching a speedbag while trainers yell at them and call them names, impromptu matches in the ring that ends up with someone being knocked out, countless taunts and insults. The usual.

But that wasn't the case here. Yes, it's in a warehouse on the outskirts of the city, but inside I'm surprised to find it bright and airy. There aren't many people about, just a couple sparring in one area while another grapples with each other on a wide mat, like a mild version of UFC.

"So this is where the magic happens," I say to Lachlan.

He grunts something in return while shooting me a humble smile. I know he likes to downplay himself but he's been boxing for quite a while now and knowing the way he throws himself into something 100 per cent, he's going to be good.

And he is.

I sit down on a bench while his trainer, Jake, comes out and introduces himself to me. I think I was expecting Ernest Borgnine, you know, fat and old, ready for Rocky, maybe even Nick Nolte. But he's younger than both of us, very Scottish and surprisingly tanned.

Lachlan talks to him for a moment about things I can't quite hear or understand and then takes off his shirt, unveiling that taught, toned torso and all those tattoos. He adorns boxing gloves and heads off toward a punching bag in the corner, listening intently to every word his trainer is telling him.

I don't think I've seen a sexier sight than watching Lachlan have a mean, hard go at the punching bag. I mean, I'm not sure how that can even be possible after last night, or maybe life with Lachlan in general, but at the moment it's true. He's completely in the zone, that brow of his furrowed in deep concentration as he hits the bag over and over. It's like nothing else exists for him and he gives every ounce of himself, his muscles taught like strung wires, sweat pouring down his forehead and body. He hits with so much force I can practically feel it shake my bones.

He's only with his trainer for about 45-minutes, some of it sparring, some of it doing sit-ups and kicks, but it's more than enough. When he's done, he grabs a towel and starts wiping his brow, sauntering over to me. His smile, his eyes, everything about him is relaxed, so similar to the way he is after sex.

"You," I start to say, running my fingers over his shoulders, down his arms, not caring about the sweat one bit. "You were amazing."

He gives me a dry look. "I was weak today. I've been quicker."

I shake my head. "You have no idea, do you?"

He frowns at me and picks up a bottle of water, quickly screwing off the top before downing it. Nope. He has no idea at all what an amazing man he really is. His ego wouldn't even let that fact settle in.

Lachlan opts to hit the showers back at home, so we get in his car and are about to drive off when he gets a text from Thierry, his rugby teammate and friend, wanting to go out.

"He wants to go to the Christmas market tonight," Lachlan says. "But I'm okay with telling him no. We have a lot on our plate."

I like Thierry, even though I never got a chance to know him that well. He's French and oh so handsome and charming. But more than that, I like seeing Lachlan around his friends, just as long as we don't end up hanging out at a pub. I can tell though, that this is why Thierry suggested the market. It's neutral ground and even if we were there last night, I don't mind going back. It's Christmas, after all.

"It's fine," I assure him. "Really. Maybe this time we can go on the damn Ferris wheel."

However, when we go to the market later that night to meet Thierry, the line is just as long as before.

"How about ice skating?" Thierry suggests, nodding in the direction of the ice rink which looks equally as packed.

Here's the thing about ice skating. I hate it. My balance is pretty non-existent, which was one reason why I used to do my fencing lessons back in San Francisco – it helped stabilize me. The one time I made it onto the ice, back when I was in grade school, I spent the whole time on my ass, while my crush, Billy Ga-Ga Green, made fun of me. It was mortifying and I never went skating again. Nor did I talk to Billy ever again.

But I'm not about to tell Lachlan this, even though he's eying me intently in that way that makes you want to give up all of your secrets.

"Not a fan?" he asks.

I give him and Thierry a tight smile. I don't want to seem whiney and no fun, especially in front of his friend. "I'm just not very good at it," I say simply.

"Well I'll tell you something," Lachlan says, lowering his voice and leaning in slightly, his breath hot on my cheek, "I'm not very good either."

"Bullshit. You're good at everything."

"No, it's true," Thierry says quickly, his Parisian accent making it sound so dramatic. "Believe him. The team had to do a photoshoot with us skating once and Lachlan was terrible. Just terrible."

Lachlan rolls his eyes. "It didn't help that you were a figure skater in a past life."

Thierry shrugs, shooting him a sly smile. "No need to be jealous."

As we make our way down to the rink and I begrudgingly shove on a pair of rented skates that smell like they've been made of cheese, I realize that Thierry really can skate like an angel and contrary to Lachlan's self-effacing attitude and the Frenchman's claims, Lachlan is the opposite of terrible.

I mean, he's not the best of the best but he can at least stand on the ice and move smoothly without eating shit every five seconds. Not like me.

By the time I fall down for the tenth time, Lachlan shakes his head and hoists me to my feet.

"Kayla, I hate to tell you this," Lachlan says earnestly, holding my hands. "But you might just be complete rubbish at this."

"I told you!" I exclaim, wanting to hit him but knowing that if I let go of him for a second I would fall again.

Thierry skates over to us. "Actually I believe she said she wasn't very good at it. That implied that she would be somewhat good. Which she is not."

"Ferme la bouche," I tell Thierry. *Shut your mouth.*

He raises his brow, folding his hands behind his back. "I better get out of here before she uses more French on me. Somehow it's worse than her skating."

Thierry quickly skates away and I yell after him, "You know, you don't need to talk about me like I'm not here!"

"He means well," Lachlan says, his eyes twinkling even more so with the reflection of the white rink. "As well as a Frenchman can. Come on. Let's get you around the rink at least once."

Before I can protest, Lachlan comes around me, his skates on the insides of mine, one arm wrapped around my waist, the other holding onto my arm.

"Just like this," he whispers into my ear and my nerves dance along my neck, down my limbs, alighting my body like only he can.

I'm as tense as anything, my legs starting to shake as he slowly glides forward, pushing me with him. I know I'm going to bail at any moment.

But Lachlan's body is so strong, so powerful, so solid against mine. And when he whispers into my ear, "I've got you," I believe him. He has me – now and forever. He won't ever let go. He won't ever let me fall.

I relax, closing my eyes, and let myself sink into his warmth, his mass. I let my worries melt away and just become one with his heartbeats, his movements, as much as possible. It's almost like sex in that way, that our bodies are so fine-tuned to each other, our connection is nothing short of second nature.

We glide so effortlessly, my hair blowing back from my face, the chill of the wind on my nose and cheeks, it almost feels like a snow-dusted Christmas dream.

"Open your eyes," Lachlan whispers.

I do and see that we are already on the other side of the rink. It felt like we got here through no effort at all.

"I can't believe it," I say softly, looking across the crowded rink.

"You better. You had this in you. Sometimes we just need to have a little faith and try again."

Boy is he right about that.

"Want to keep skating?" he asks me.

"Only if we can skate all night," I tell him.

I lean back against his chest, his big arms around me, and we slow dance on ice, me and my beast.

CHAPTER FOUR

Lachlan

"Are you ready?" I call out for Kayla. I know Emily, Jo and Lionel are, Emily in her crate while the others sit at my feet, tails thumping with no idea where we are going.

"Just a minute," I hear her say. It's followed by a whole heap of rattling coming from the bedroom. I know she's been fretting all morning over what to pack for Christmas, even though it's not like she came here with a lot of options.

Finally she emerges, lugging her suitcase instead of her overnight duffel bag that she had before.

"It's just for a few nights," I gently remind her, sticking my hand out, offering to take it.

She holds it back from me. "I couldn't decide. Everything I own just doesn't seem good enough."

I can see the glimmer of fear in her eyes. It softens me, inside out.

"Listen, love," I tell her. "There is absolutely nothing for you to worry about. You are good enough. Bloody hell, you're far too good for me. You know Jessica and Donald love you and they won't ever do anything but love you...that's just how they are."

"But I haven't seen them since I moved back here. I don't know, what if they think I'm totally crazy now, you know, for coming here?"

I can't help but smile. "Well, I assure you they already think you're a bit nuts. I mean, you are with me after all."

"I'm serious," she says, adjusting her grip on the suitcase until I take it from her.

"I know you are. It's going to be fine."

At least, I'm hoping it will be. I know they all love her and are especially excited for her to spend Christmas with us. It's just George that I'm still a bit worried about. And I know she feels the same way.

"And your grandfather?" she asks, right on target.

I look away, wiggling my lower jaw as I search for the right words. "Take anything he says with a grain of salt. We all do."

Except for me, of course. But I'm still learning.

Eventually we get all our luggage and the dogs into the car, stopping by my friend Amara's flat first. Normally I bring at least Lionel with me everywhere, if not Emily and Jo, but George is decidedly against dogs. That should tip you off about his character right there. One time I brought Lionel and he would barely let me in the house. I spent an hour having tea and then left back for Edinburgh right away. I won't be making that mistake again, not now.

Maybe this isn't a very macho thing to admit, but whenever I say goodbye to the dogs it gets a bit emotional. They always know what's up and even though they have a good time with Amara, it pulls at my heart to see their sad eyes, hear that whine.

Naturally, it puts me in a pensive mood for our drive to Aberdeen. I'm barely noticing the way the snow deepens, how charming the landscape becomes, until Kayla gasps and taps me on the arm.

"A castle!" she exclaims, turning to look at me with wide eyes. "Can we go?"

I look up, missing the sign she must have seen. Still, we're about a half hour south of Aberdeen and close to the coast and Dunottar Castle.

"You mean Dunottar?" I ask.

"Yes, I think," she says. "I mean, if it's not much trouble."

Nothing would be too much trouble when it comes to her and I'm certainly in no hurry to get to Aberdeen now that this dark mood has found me. Besides, it has been ages since I'd last been to a castle.

I take the next exit and soon we find ourselves standing on the wind blasted cliffs at Dunottar Castle. There is no snow here at the moment, just an endless green that swoops down to the roaring sea. It somehow feels colder here than anywhere else and I instinctively put my arm around Kayla, holding her tight as her scarf whips around her.

"This is like out of a movie," she says in awe, taking it all in. "Or Game of Thrones."

"Actually," I tell her proudly, "the movie Hamlet with Mel Gibson was shot here."

And it's easy to see why. The castle is perched on a part of the cliffs that juts out to sea, providing only a narrow isthmus as a walkway to the castle. As we make our way down the path and across the narrow neck to the sprawling, crumbling castle walls, it's easy to see how back in the day this place was naturally protected against enemies. With high cliffs that plunge to the sea nearly surrounding the whole thing, it's as good as an island.

There are a lot of steps leading down from the carpark and across to the castle and a few times the wind comes at us as if it's trying to knock us off the path, an age old protector of the ruins. In fact when we pay for our tickets, the woman warns us that they might have to close the castle early due to the high winds.

We try to make it quick, but this place beckons for you to stay and explore as long as possible. We start around the edges and work our way in, walking along the perfectly groomed lawns that lead toward the remains of the buildings. Surprisingly, visitors are allowed in the buildings, even though they look like they're about to crumble on you.

Kayla has her phone out as we walk, taking pictures of everything. At one point the wind whips her scarf off and I manage to snatch it out of the air before it blows over to the sea.

"Let's go inside," I tell her, loud enough to be heard over the wind and roaring waves, just as her phone rings.

She nods, staring down at the screen. She grimaces and looks up at me with wide eyes. I can barely hear her. "It's about the job!"

I swallow, my heart thudding a few beats as she answers the call, plugging up her other ear with her finger. I can only hope that this is good news – Kayla really has had her heart set on the writing position. I know that even without it, she'll find something else and with Ruff Love, there are always work opportunities. She'll be more than okay. But obviously I want her happy above anything.

I watch as she walks away from me and under the crumbling stone doorway into the nearest building. She keeps her back to me, walking past a family who are peering at a map in the dimness. She keeps walking until she reaches a wall and then nods a few times.

Even though the wind is kept out of the castle walls, I still can't hear her very well. I stay back though, not wanting to intrude when she's talking about a private matter, even though I want her to know I'm there for her.

Finally she hangs up the phone, slowly sliding it into her coat pocket, and from the way her shoulders fall, I know it's not good news. She didn't get it.

"Kayla," I say gently, even though I'm not sure she can hear me. I go over to her, hovering at her back briefly before placing my hand on her shoulder. "Are you okay?"

She nods and I hear her sniff. It bloody breaks my heart already. She then turns around and though she isn't crying, her eyes are soft and wavering.

"That, uh," she says quietly. She clears her throat. "That was 24 Hours. I didn't get the job."

"I'm so sorry," I tell her, trying to pull her into a hug, though her body is stiff. "I know how much you wanted it."

"Yeah," she says with a sigh, nodding against me.

"But you know you'll be okay, right? You know that. I'll take care of you."

Obviously I've said the wrong thing because she stiffens up even more and pulls back.

"I don't need you to take care of me," she snaps. "I needed that job."

I can only nod. I hate feeling hopeless around her. More than that, I hate that she's worrying and fretting about something she doesn't need to. Her pride is just as strong as mine is, which is both a blessing and a curse. Times like this though, I wish she'd give in. Just a little. There's nothing shameful about taking help when it's offered to you, especially when it comes from someone who loves you, who only wants what's best. Fuck, it took me a long time to grapple with that fact myself and it wasn't until I saw that Kayla and Brigs had the best intentions for my own sake that I knew what I had to do to help myself.

"I know," I tell her. "They're complete wankers for not hiring you."

She manages to give me a faint smile. She always smiles when I use that word. But the smile quickly fades and she shakes her head, walking past me and through the cold, damp ruins of the castle.

I follow, grabbing her hand, letting her know I'm there for her. She keeps walking, as if leading me and we wind our way through the structure in silence. The wind outside is picking up and I'm about to mention that maybe we should make our way back to the car when she suddenly grabs me as we turn a corner, pulling me into a darkened room with a slit for a window and an uneven, rocky floor.

She brings me to her, her back against the wall. Her hands go to my face, fingers so soft and cold, and stares at me, her eyes searching mine through a million different feelings and I'm torn in a million different ways, grasping for something to say that will make her feel better.

"There will be other jobs," I say feebly but I can tell from the fire in her eyes that she doesn't want to hear it.

"It doesn't matter," she says. She pulls my face down to hers and kisses me, hard, deep, as if she's suddenly afraid that she won't survive without my lips on hers, my tongue lost in her warmth. We kiss as if we aren't standing among the ruins of an old castle, the wind battering the stone walls, the cold slicing through the cracks, the deafening roar of the waves as they crash against the coast. We certainly aren't behaving like there are tourists milling about in the other rooms, especially not as Kayla's hands slip over my dick, pressing hard against my firm length and coaxing a deep moan from me.

This is about her distraction now, not mine.

I will gladly do what I can.

I move away from her hands and undo the button on her jeans before unzipping them. I pull them down to the ground and her thong along with it.

"What are you doing?" she whispers.

I kiss her hard and then drop to my knees. Without saying a word, I start licking up her cold, bare, naked thighs until she shivers and moans, until goosebumps erupt all over her delicate flesh. I slide my fingers into her pussy, wet and wanting despite the circumstances. She's practically melting into my touch and I melt into her.

Once she begins breathing hard, swaying her hips for more, I keep her pressed back against the castle wall and bring up one of her legs, hooking it over my shoulder. She grabs the top of my head for stability, her fingers sinking into my hair as I leave soft, wet kisses from the side of her knee all the way up her inner thigh. My lips and tongue tease her mercilessly, one of my favorite things to do.

Her body tenses and relaxes from my touch, and I grab hold of the sides of her hips, hard, as I bring my face between her legs. My lips meet her swollen ones and I tease her clit with the tip of my finger before sliding my tongue along her cleft and plunging it inside her.

Jesus.

So hot, so tight, so wet.

She's nothing short of a tonic.

Her exquisite, heady taste dances on my tongue, reaching deep inside of me and igniting this primal layer, the caveman at my center. I want to devour her until there's nothing left. I want to make her scream and squirm and moan into oblivion.

I want to be all there is for her.

She cries out, her fist in my hair hard as she sinks further into me, hips rocking for pressure, for purchase. I give it all, my fingers going in deeper, sliding along the right places, my tongue working her clit overtime until she's nothing short of a ripe pear, juices running down my chin.

I'm not sure I can ever get enough of her. Of this.

I'm doomed in the most maddening way.

She's close to coming now and I swear, somewhere in the distance, beyond the crashing waves and the wind, I can hear a woman yelling that the castle is closing early.

It doesn't matter. Kayla's already done.

She comes hard into my mouth, her clit pulsing beneath my lips, and I drink her all in, keeping her coming until she moans for me to stop.

I pull my head away and look up at her serene, pleasured face, wiping my lips with the back of my hand.

"You scratch my back, I scratch yours," I say thickly.

She smiles at me, then her eyes flit over my shoulder and widen.

"Hey, what's going on in here!" a woman yells and I turn around to see the woman who took our tickets looking at us through the window, face red and sweaty and somehow angered by what she's just seen.

"Bloody hell," I cry out as I scamper to my knees and help Kayla yank up her pants. I grab her hand and we start running through the castle, looking for a way out in which we won't run into her.

We nearly trip over a ledge but then we turn a corner and a doorway opens up to the expanse of green lawn. The two of us run like hell across it, all the way to the walkway and to the car.

We don't even have time to catch our breath. We get into the car and burn off, leaving the castle in our dust. It isn't until we get onto the highway that we both start laughing our arses off.

That's probably the last time we'll ever be allowed at Dunottar Castle, but dear god, it was worth it.

CHAPTER FIVE

Kayla

I can totally understand why people become sex addicts. Or any addicts really. But mainly the sex part. The wonderful endorphins that float through your veins and that warm, smooth feeling of "everything's going to be all right" that only an orgasm high can bring had lasted from the walk (well, we were running from the woman, let's be honest) to the car, for the next thirty minutes and all the way through Lachlan's mini-tour of the city of Aberdeen.

It lasted while I *ooohed* and *ahhhed* over the stone buildings, the uniform look of the city houses and streets, how utterly charming and festive it all looked dressed up in Christmas gear. That feeling of peace was centered inside me. Like all the sharp claws you sometimes feel dragging you down from the inside out had been polished down to shiny nubs.

But the high – that beautiful distraction – only lasts so long. And as Lachlan drives us out of the city and we pull down a long country lane to his grandfather's house, I'm back to being a neurotic mess and then some. It's not just that I've been extremely nervous about spending Christmas with his family, wondering how they really view me, if they'll really accept me, particularly the grandpa, it's having to deal with the crushing blow from earlier.

I think in the back of my head I kind of knew I wouldn't get the job. I don't know why but it was always there, this niggling feeling that things wouldn't work out so easily. After all, I'm here on a visitor's visa and technically can't work anyway. But even so, it didn't stop me from being utterly disappointed and let-down. I just thought that if I got it, it would solidify that I made the right choice to come here. It would mean that I was better off, not only being with the man I love but with a career I've always wanted.

Now though, I'm back to feeling those doubts about everything. I know I'll be okay and in the end I know Lachlan will take care of me, but I just really wanted that as the last resort. But the doubt over my career is still there. I don't want to just work somewhere to work somewhere. I've spent most of my adult life doing that. I want a career. I want to finally be a part of something that I believe in, that I'm good at.

And of course, no one likes to feel rejected. I don't take it very well. And apparently all the hot castle sex in the world isn't enough to erase the fact that I, Kayla Moore, just wasn't good for that newspaper. What happens if this is only the first of many rejections? What if I'm not good enough for any company in this country, regardless if I'm allowed to work here? What if I'm not good enough for this country at all?

"Easy, love," Lachlan says to me gently as he squeezes my hand, the car coming to a stop in front of a picturesque stone house with a wreath on the door. "You're going to do fine."

Whether he means with his family or my career, I don't know, but I'll take either one at this point.

I exhale slowly and try and calm down, forcing my brain into a different space. I concentrate on the fact that at least his grandfather lives in a very magical place.

All around the house are sloping fields, covered with a deep layer of snow. In the sunlight it sparkles like insane glitter, nearly burning your eyes as the world around you lights up like the heavens. The house itself looks quite old though it's very well taken care of, from the glossy finish of the wood door, to the way the window panes shine. Lachlan tells me it's been in the McGregor family for centuries and it's the right thing to say because suddenly I'm marveling at how old everything is over here, how much history there is between simple walls, especially when compared to America. Suddenly I feel a flash of gratitude and excitement that I took the chance to come over here.

With the snow crunching beneath our boots, we gather our gifts from the backseat and I cringe at the way I did mine late last night. The best I could, but still a bit crooked and lumpy, with mismatched tape.

Before we can make it to the front door, it swings open and Jessica comes rushing out, throwing on a coat as she comes.

"Let me help you," she says in her adorable brogue, hands out to take some gifts from Lachlan's hands but he playfully shoos her away. She comes to me smiling. "Kayla, I'm so glad you're here," she says before pulling me into a quick embrace, my nose filling with scents of jasmine and amber.

Jessica is stunning, the type of woman I want to be when I'm her age. Her skin is flawless, her makeup subtle, her sleek grey bob done just so while her all-black pantsuit under the camel coat looks effortless and chic. Even the velvet slippers she seems to have shoved on to come outside look elegant on her.

"Thank you for inviting me over for Christmas," I tell her, straightening my shoulders and trying to look somewhat respectable. For a horrifying moment I'm afraid that maybe my shirt is unbuttoned or my fly is down or I have pieces of castle dirt and dust in my hair and I wait until I'm following them into the house to check. So far, so good. Though now, of course, I'm blushing at my memories.

In the foyer Donald is waiting, holding a steaming mug and smiling wryly at us. He looks a lot like Brigs, maybe even Bram, and has this very professional, unassuming way about him.

"You made it," he says to us and though his voice is stern, his eyes behind his glasses are soft. "Thought we'd have to send out a search party."

"Sorry," Lachlan says, giving him a hug. I get such a kick out watching this big, hulking, tatted man embrace his prim and proper adopted father. "I wanted to take her to Dunottar Castle."

"Oooh," Jessica says, taking my presents from me as I pull off my coat. "What a special place. Must have been very cold though, that wind."

"Actually it was fine. Even quite hot at times," Lachlan says casually and I can feel my face going red again. I quickly turn to hang up my coat. Normally I don't get bashful over innuendos but around his parents is a whole other story.

We make our way into the rest of the house, which is slightly more modern than the outside and bigger than I thought. The floors are carpeted with dense, patterned rugs, ones that maybe Jessica picked out. They seem her style and I have no problems believing she may have had a hand in decorating the place.

There are pastoral paintings of Scottish landscapes on the walls, framed by deep wood and antique side tables crammed with photos. I pause, glancing them over. In one picture I see Brigs in his graduate attire, probably from when he got his masters or PhD. I see a faded photo from the eighties of two young boys in school uniforms, one with golden brown hair, the taller one with dark, cheeky smiles on both of them.

Lachlan nudges me.

"Linden and Bram," he says.

I smile and decide to take a picture of it later to send to Stephanie and Nicola.

Funnily enough though, I don't see any pictures of Lachlan, at least not at first glance. I thought perhaps Lachlan was exaggerating about the way his relationship with his grandfather is but maybe not.

We're ushered into the kitchen, a nice homey room with a low ceiling and a brick backsplash where Jessica hands us mugs of mulled wine with cinnamon stick stirrers.

"No thanks, I'm okay," Lachlan declines, his shoulders stiffening.

"It's non-alcoholic," she says brightly. "From IKEA." She picks up a bottle of the stuff from beside a simmering pot on the stove and waves it at us.

Lachlan visibly relaxes and takes a sip. Honestly, I'm so jumpy and nervous right now that I'd love to spike mine with something but if Lachlan can handle it, so can I.

"Where's George?" Lachlan asks.

Jessica nods upstairs. "He says he didn't sleep well last night. He's taking a nap."

I have to admit, I breathe out a sigh of relief at that.

"Come on, let's go into the drawing room," Jessica says. "You two must be starving. I spent the last two days baking but only one batch wasn't complete rubbish."

We head into the drawing room, which is warm and welcoming with Christmas music, a giant, gorgeous tree, and an ancient-looking stone fireplace complete with stockings and a roaring fire. Lachlan and I settle into a worn leather couch, adorned with throws while Jessica shows off the spread on the coffee table. Christmas cookies that look so unbelievably perfect that I can scarcely believe she made them, mini crustless sandwiches and scones with clotted cream adorn the table, along with a pot of tea and fine china.

"Jessica," Lachlan says to her. "It's just us. You really shouldn't have."

"Oh, it's all for Brigs," Donald quips and we laugh.

"When is he coming here?" I ask.

"Not until tomorrow," Jessica says. "He's driving up in the afternoon."

"Well he better get that car of his prepared," Donald says. "If it snows again, he's going to be in some trouble."

"What kind of car is it?" I ask, having never seen Brigs' car.

"It's gorgeous is what it is," Lachlan says to me. "Though far too high maintenance for me. After all, I already have you," he adds slyly.

I love it when he puts his brooding attitude away and starts to joke. I manage to refrain from smacking his arm. "You jerk."

"Brigs has had the car forever," Donald says, adjusting his glasses. "It's a 1978 Aston Martin."

"That's a James Bond car!" I exclaim.

"Yes, well, James wouldn't drive this one," Lachlan says. "It's a V-8 but it runs like a tired old horse. It gets him around and looks pretty but the thing ends up in the shop once a week. He rarely drives it now."

"Though I do think if his new teaching position falls through, he can always get work as a mechanic at this point," Donald says.

"So you know now," Lachlan says to them. "That he's moving to London."

Jessica and Donald exchange a look before Jessica says quietly, "He told us the other day. It will be a shame to not have him so close but...he needs this. He really does. He needs to put everything behind him and I just don't think he can do that until he moves on, even if just to another city."

Donald nods. "Besides, we love London. We might end up taking the train down every weekend. Poor boy might see us more than he does now."

Watching them talk about Brigs and all he's gone through, not to mention everything that Lachlan has had to endure, really hits home that this family has walked through their share of fire. It makes me realize that perhaps the last thing they are judging is me and I shouldn't be so worked up over it. I think Jessica and Donald are just happy that their two sons are doing so well now, crawling out of the mounds of ashes and into the light. At least, that's what I'm going to keep reminding myself.

"So, Kayla," Jessica says, turning her bright eyes over to me. "How are you finding the transition over to Scotland? Does it feel any different now that you're going to stay?"

"Definitely," I tell her. "Of course, I can only stay here for six months and then I have to figure out a visa."

"But we'll figure that out when the time comes," Lachlan fills in, putting his hand on my knee. "Kayla's grandfather on her father's side was born in England before he moved to Iceland, so we may be able to get her a UK ancestry visa if nothing else."

"Well, well, well." A low, strong brogue just shy of Groundskeeper Willie sounds out from behind us and I crane my neck to see George McGregor standing in the doorway. "I guess you decided to show."

Lachlan's grandfather is exactly what I thought he would be. Tall, but hunched over. Thick white hair. Furry eyebrows. Glasses. A permanent scowl. Old man cardigan and hiked-up pants. A cane which seems more for ornamental use than mobility. Even though he's ancient, there's something about him that makes me sit up straighter.

"George," Lachlan says to him with a polite nod. "Thank you for having us for Christmas. This is Kayla."

I try and give him my most charming smile and hold out my hand, but he doesn't even look my way, keeps shuffling toward the empty armchair beside Jessica. "Thank her," he says gruffly, pointing at Jessica. "She's the one who thought this was a good idea." He settles into his chair, folding his hands across his lap. "I would have been perfectly happy with just me and the boys down at the Lions club for dinner, maybe Christmas mass too."

"Oh hush," Jessica says and for once I see her looking a little less composed. "Of course you're going to spend Christmas with family." She pauses. "Lachlan here was trying to introduce you to Kayla, his girlfriend."

Finally, the old man looks at me. He squints and his scowl deepens. "Oh is that who that is. I thought you brought me a new nurse. Like that Vietnamese one I once had."

I swallow hard and keep the fake smile pasted on my face. "It's nice to meet you," I say loudly, in case he can't hear well.

"No need to shout, I'm not deaf," he grumbles. "So you're the one who moved here for this guy, is that so?" He gestures to Lachlan with a wave of his hand.

"I did," I tell him, shaking just slightly. "I love Scotland."

"That's just what we need," he says. "Another immigrant from a foreign country."

"She's American," Lachlan says, a hard edge to his voice. "She's born and raised in San Francisco."

"And America is a foreign country, is it not?" His grandfather challenges him back. He nudges Jessica. "Jessy, fix me up a plate."

Jessica nods and busies herself putting together a plate of cookies and appetizers from the table. Silence falls across the room as she does so and I can hear Lachlan breathing heavily, probably trying to control his temper. He gets really defensive over me, especially when it comes to the fact I'm half Japanese. I admire him for it, but the last thing I want is for him to fight his grandfather.

I put my hand on his back and rub his strained muscles, wishing we were back in that castle, or back in bed at home. Anywhere but here, really. But I smile for him anyway, refusing to let him think anything is bothering me. I'm a big girl, I can handle it.

"So what work do you do?" George says through a mouthful of cookie, crumbs shooting out every which way.

Oh, just the right question to ask.

"Well, I, uh," I start to say. "I'm a writer. I was hoping to get a job here in that field."

He laughs unkindly. "Good luck with that. You think you can just get a job like that? Get in line with all the people who are actually UK citizens, born and raised, who need work and can't get it. You think you'll get something? You're better off cleaning houses."

I can feel my face flaming up. I don't even have a rebuttal because what he's saying is totally true and my worst fear.

"Actually," Lachlan says, stepping to my defense again. "Kayla is extremely smart and talented, more so than half the tossers in this country. If anything else, she'll be a worthy addition to Ruff Love."

"Ruff what?" he asks, frowning in total old person exaggeration.

Lachlan sighs while Jessica says, "Ruff Love. Lachlan's organization, the shelter for the dogs."

"Bah," he says. "They're better left on the streets. You know what they say about dogs? They're for people who need love because they can't get it anywhere else. Dogs are just retarded children with fur." He takes a sip of his tea and grimaces. "Christ, Jessy. How long did you steep this for?"

Lachlan is so tense beside me, his eyes taking on that wild, hardened look I fear that any moment he's just going to reach across the table, grab his grandfather by the throat and throttle him. And when he gets up, for a second I think that's just what he's going to do. But he looks down at me, attempts a half-smile and says, "We should go put our stuff away in our room. We might be too tired later."

Thank fucking god. An out.

I get up quickly and we hustle out of the room while Donald calls out after us, "You're in the usual room."

We grab our bags from the foyer and then head up the creaky wooden stairs to the second floor. Once we are out of sight from the drawing room, Lachlan stops and leans his head against the wall, eyes closed, and breathes in and out deeply. I watch him for a few moments until he straightens up, the line between his eyes softening, and nods at the open door closest to us.

"That's our room."

I go inside, putting the bag on the floor and he closes the door behind us. I absently take in the space – the wood floor, the cornflower blue walls and matching bedspread, the window sill dusted with snow – but my mind is still reeling over everything that happened downstairs.

All I can say is, "Wow." I sit down on the bed, the mattress overly soft.

Lachlan nods, rubbing his hand over his jaw. I can hear the bristle of his stubble. "Yeah. Wow is right. He just hit up all the things I love in a matter of seconds."

"I'm sorry," I tell him, wringing my hands together.

"No," he says emphatically, leaning down and placing his hands on my shoulders, his pained green eyes searching mine. "I'm sorry. He had no right to speak to you that way."

I run my fingers along his cheekbone, down the side of his cheek, to his lips. "Lachlan, please. I know it has nothing to do with you. I'm a tough cookie. I can handle it. He's pretty much your typical grandpa. Maybe a bit more racist than most but otherwise just a grumpy old man." I close my eyes and kiss him softly, sweetly. "Really. Don't worry about me."

But I know he does. He can't help himself.

We stay in the room for a while, slowly putting our clothes away and tucking presents underneath the bed. He tells me this used to be his uncle's room (Linden and Bram's father). His father's old room is next door, where Brigs will be staying and his aunt's old room is where Jessica and Donald are. I can tell we're just trying to waste time before going back downstairs but we can't hide forever.

When we finally do go downstairs though, the grandfather is nowhere to be found and Jessica is puttering around, putting away dishes.

"Where is everyone?" Lachlan asks as we step into the kitchen and she nearly jumps.

"They went for a walk," Jessica says, hustling over to us. She takes us both by the arms and leads us back into the drawing room. "Here, sit by the fire. Relax, I'll bring you some tea."

Our protests don't seem to matter and Jessica doesn't mention anything to do with George, so Lachlan and I settle in our seats, still on edge, waiting for the grandfather and Donald to come back in, while "Silver Bells" plays from the speakers.

When they do come back though, George is remarkably silent. I'm going to assume the walk he took with Donald was to get him to de-grumpify. The rest of the evening actually goes along quite well and when everyone gathers around the fire before dinner, for what I assume is their usual cocktail hour, both Jessica and Donald stick to the alcohol-free mulled wine, while George sips from a tiny glass of Sherry. I know it's got to help Lachlan that barely anyone is drinking.

After small talk – rugby and politics – we retire to the kitchen for dinner, with Jessica whipping together a chicken casserole dish that didn't turn into mush like most casserole does.

In fact, it reminds me of my mother and the terrible casserole she used to make when I was young. While Jessica's is creamy and fragrant with sprigs of rosemary, my mother's was the gelatinous glob of grey mushroom soup goo. Everyone except Toshio and me ate it up. We were the picky ones and after a while it became a running joke that Toshio and I would starve on casserole nights.

Terrible cooking or not, the memories hit me like a sledgehammer.

Fuck. *Fuck.*

I miss my mom.

I miss her, deeply, terribly, with every cell inside me.

I wish she was here. I wish my dad was here too. My brothers. I wish I could just have a normal Christmas with everyone but nothing hurts more than the cold hard truth that that will never happen. Sure, maybe next year I can go back to California and see my brothers but nothing will ever bring our parents back, no matter how hard we wish for it. They say your wishes come true at Christmas time but this one definitely won't.

Lachlan leans into me, whispering in my ear, "You okay?"

I want to nod. But I can't. If I do, tears will spill down my cheek. So I just get up as calmly and quickly as possible and head to the toilet. Once inside, I wet a towel and dab it all over my face, as if cold water will shock away all my grief and sadness.

I want to let it all out, to bawl and just be sad, be alone in my sorrow. But I can't, not now. I know most people would understand, but I'm just not comfortable here. So I suck it all up, bury it deep down, brush my hair back from my face and put on my most winning smile.

I go back out and enjoy the rest of the dinner, even making small talk, though George won't look my way at all. I don't mind.

Later that night, Lachlan and I retire to our bed early. We don't even have sex for once, I just feel too tired, too lost in my head and while the distraction from earlier today worked wonders while it lasted, I can't even entertain the idea now.

But Lachlan is forever the gentleman. As we climb into the tiny, creaking bed with thin covers, he holds me to his hard frame until I feel the beating of his heart at my back. It's a rhythm, along with his steady breaths, that brings me into a dark, solid sleep.

When we wake up the next morning, it's snowing. Everything has been wiped clean.

CHAPTER SIX

Lachlan

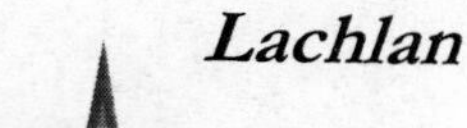

"It's snowing," Kayla says, her voice entering my dreams until my eyes flutter open.

For a hot second I don't know where I am, the world seems blue and white and the mattress beneath me is sagging toward the middle, making me think I'm in a hammock in the sky. Then I remember. My grandfather's house. Here to fight another day.

But at least it's Christmas Eve and Brigs should be showing up later to share some of the pressure from my family. I've got the woman of my heart in bed beside me. And, outside the window, flakes of snow are falling from the sky. The white Christmas so many wish for? Well, we've got it.

I rub at my face, attempting to sit up. The air is decidedly chilly outside the blanket. "What time is it?"

"Eight-thirty," she says.

I groan. I slept in. I promised myself I would stick to my schedules of getting up at the crack of dawn and exercising. Though by the looks of it, my idea of going for a run has been buried by the snowfall.

I slowly get out of bed and invite Kayla to take a shower with me. She declines, feeling uneasy in the house and I can't really blame her. After yesterday she's more fragile than ever. The way my grandfather was with her, her losing out on the job, not to mention I know she's really feeling the loss of her mother right now – it's all adding up.

As we get ready for the day, though, I feel I better force some Christmas cheer down my throat before Jessica does it for me.

"You ready, love?" I ask her, kissing the palm of her hand.

"With you? Always."

Hand in hand we head down the stairs and find ourselves in a scene from a Christmas movie.

It's early but Jessica has been doing the rounds, cooking up a storm and filling the house with a mix of mouth-watering scents. A few more Christmas decorations have appeared, including mistletoe over the doorframe, and the music is loud and cheery.

She greets us, wiping her hands on her festive apron. "Morning. Merry Christmas Eve! What would you two like to eat?"

The both of us aren't picky eaters and I tell her we're fine with just toast and orange marmalade but Jessica won't have any of that. She fries up a real Scottish breakfast of beans, eggs, mushrooms, half a tomato, ham, *tattie* scones, sausage and black pudding (which Kayla won't even touch, now that she knows what it is), along with orange juice and endless pots of tea. By the time breakfast is over, I feel like climbing back into bed. The comatose feeling is a nice change from anxiety though.

Even though last night everything went fine and everyone behaved themselves, with George only having a bit of sherry earlier, there was still this thread of tension that felt like it ran from me to everyone in the house. I know Kayla can feel it, I know everyone else does too. Everyone is tip-toeing around me like I'm a rocket that can accidently fire. Maybe George doesn't quite know yet, or maybe he does and doesn't care, but no one wants to be responsible for my downfall and I just want to tell everyone that I appreciate it but they don't have to worry about me.

I worry about myself enough as it is.

After we're done in the kitchen, we put our presents under the tree. George is in his favorite chair, acknowledging us with only a grunt. I guess it could be worse. Then Kayla and I go outside for a long walk and to bask in the snowfall.

It's the right decision. Not only does it get us in the Christmas spirit, but Kayla is like a little kid, going nuts with her tongue stuck out, trying to catch snowflakes. We make our way over to the fallow field next door which belongs to a farmer a kilometer away. In summer it's overgrown and reedy but now it's a blanket of white. It beckons to either be photographed in its pristine condition or to be ravaged.

We decide to ravage it.

With Kayla calling the shots, we make snowmen and snow dogs. She attempts to make Lionel, Emily and Jo but they look like lumpy white logs instead. Then I pelt her in the head with a snowball, completely blasting her with snow all over her face.

She shrieks and a snowball war ensues with both of us hiding behind our snow creatures. Needless to say, I have pretty good aim, so I get her in the head every single time. Sometimes it's right on top, sometimes it explodes at her temple, sending ice down her coat, sometimes it pops her on the forehead. It's enough to drive her crazy and I feel like I'm harnessing the childhood I missed out on. I don't think any kid, though, could have had this much fun.

Finally we cap it off by making snow angels, before trudging back to the house wet, cold and absolutely exhausted. But fuck, have I never seen a more beautiful sight than Kayla with her hair wet around her face, her dark eyes bright, her cheeks and nose flushed pink from the outdoors. She looks utterly alive, happy, and it bolsters some reserve inside me. I shouldn't spend the rest of the day fretting about things I may not be able to control. I should be joyous as fuck that the woman of my dreams is in love with me, beside me, wanting to go through it all by my side.

I'm pretty sure that's what the holiday is all about anyway. Sure we all lose our minds a bit and go nuts with the shopping and being around family who may not always mesh well. But as long as we have those we love, nothing else really matters.

I try and keep that all in mind as the day wears on. As we dry off inside though and settle down by the fire for snacks and more tea, the world outside seems to grow darker. The wind picks up and the snow starts coming down heavier.

I glance at the clock on the wall, ticking loudly in its wood carving. "What time did Brigs say he'd leave?" I ask. Last I talked to him was last night but all he said was "See you tomorrow."

Donald gets up and stares out the window that is becoming harder to see out of. "He said he'd leave at noon. He should be here in an hour or so."

"Not in this weather, not with that damn car of his," George grumbles.

"I'm sure he'll be fine," Jessica says, though you can hear in her voice that she doesn't quite believe it.

I'm sure he'll be fine too. The car isn't as bad as we make it out to be – it's an Aston Martin after all – and I know he's got snow tires on the thing.

But after two hours of sitting by the fire, listening to Christmas music, drinking tea, snacking on cookies and making small talk about my cousin Keir who is moving back to Edinburgh after years in the army, the sky outside has fallen dark, the snow is coming down heavier and we can't pretend we aren't worried about Brigs.

"Still nothing," Jessica says, ending a call from her mobile phone and turning it over in her hands.

"His battery must be dead," I tell her as calmly as possible. "I'm sure he's on his way."

"If his battery is dead, he must be able to recharge it. Unless he can't at all," Jessica says. She blinks a million times at nothing and then scurries off into the kitchen, checking on the roast in the oven again and again.

"I should go out and see," I tell Donald, getting to my feet.

"I'm going with you," Kayla says immediately, as I knew she would.

"You're going to go find him in this?" George says, pointing at the window with his came. "Walk all the way to Edinburgh? You may play rugby Lachlan but you can't do everything."

I give him a tepid look. "We'll go to the end of the driveway, down the road maybe to the MacAuley's farm. It's better than sitting here and doing nothing."

So Kayla and I pile on the layers, coats and boots while Donald arms us with flashlights that belong with the Navy.

"Oh, don't get lost, please," Jessica says as she hovers at the door. "And turn back when you get cold. Otherwise I'll have to send Donald after you and he'll get lost right away."

I give Donald an affectionate pat on the shoulder. "We'll be right back."

I open the door and we're blasted with wind, the snowflakes slicing into our faces like shards of ice. I pull up my scarf over my nose, making sure Kayla does the same with hers, and we set out into the darkness.

Thankfully that flashlight works wonders, even though the rapidly falling snow makes visibility tricky. It's too hard to hear Kayla over the wind and crunching snow with the earmuffs and hats pulled low on our heads, so I just hold her mitted hand while we walk through a different kind of wonderland.

When we get to the end of the driveway, we scour the main rural road, looking down both ends, into nothing but blackness and driving snow. There seems to be some kind of light flickering in the distance but it's the same area as the neighboring farm. Probably a barn light. Still, I pull her hand and we set out in that direction.

Because of the snow and the wind and Kayla's short stride, it takes us a while to finally get close to the light. It does appear to be the barn and as we stop, staring at it from a few metres away, prepared to turn back, a shadow passes across the light. A human figure, seeming to walk toward us.

I lower my scarf and yell out, "Hello?" while flashing the light over. The beam keeps catching in the white of the falling flakes, throwing everything off, until finally we're just a few feet from a man.

Kayla stiffens beside me and I try to squint through the snowstorm for a better look. If it's some crazy person I can more than take care of the both of us, but most likely in this storm it's someone looking for help.

"Lachlan?"

I hear Brigs' voice and suddenly he's in front of us, his coat bundled around him and held up to his chin. He's not dressed for the weather with only his coat, a scarf and leather gloves.

"Brigs!" I exclaim, happy to see him but wondering what the hell happened. "Are you okay?"

He closes his eyes against the beam and nods. "Yes. Bloody cold but yes." He squints at me and Kayla. "Hi Kayla. I'm not far from the house am I?"

I shake my head, grabbing his arm and pulling him in the right direction. "No, we'll get you inside quick." As we trudge through the snow though, Brigs keeps his hands at his chest and collar. At first I thought he was trying to keep warm but it looks more like he's actually got something inside his coat. A present, maybe.

"What happened?" Kayla shouts at him. "Everyone was so worried."

"Bloody storm caught me by surprise. I was all right though, until just back there, at the bend near the farm. I hit a bad patch. Ended up in a snowbank. Couldn't get the car out and the MacAuleys aren't home."

"Is the car damaged?"

"She'll be fine," he says, brow furrowed against the cold. He offers me a wry smile. "Moneypenny has been through worse."

Ah, yes. I forgot he named his car. Fitting, isn't it.

We reach the start of the driveway, the journey back feeling quicker.

"I'm not alone, though," Brigs says, coming to a slow.

Kayla and I stop and look at him. He's staring at us earnestly and I scan the dark, snow-strewn world behind him. As far as I can tell, he is alone.

"What are you talking about?" I ask him, turning around. "Come on, let's talk inside."

"We can't," he says. "Because he won't be allowed inside."

I stare at him, bewildered, as Brigs undoes the top of his coat.

The small white head of a puppy pokes his head out, blinking big black eyes at the snow.

"Brigs?" I say, stepping closer, peering at the cold and frightened thing. "Where did he come from?"

He quickly closes up his coat and jerks his head toward the farm. "I was in the barn, looking for people. I heard this mewling sound, moved some hay around and found a damn puppy. Thought it was a trick of my eyes. I looked around everywhere, there wasn't another dog or any animal around. If I didn't take him, he'd freeze tonight."

"Awwww," Kayla says, practically melting at his feet. "Well hopefully he belongs to someone and they come looking for him."

"Yes, well until then it looks like he's spending the night here. And you know how our grandfather feels about dogs. Or anything cute that brings joy into people's lives."

"Oh, I know," Kayla says.

"So you've properly been introduced to old George McGregor?" Brigs asks with a raise of his brows. "Then you know. But Lachlan, you have to help me hide this thing."

"Anything for my brother, anything for a dog," I tell him.

"And your girlfriend," Kayla adds.

"Especially that," I tell her. "Come. They'll be hugging you, Mr. Popular, and the pup will get squished." I unzip my coat and put my hands out for the dog as Brigs hesitantly removes him from his coat. "While they're all praising the lord that you're alive, I'll put him up in your room.

Brigs hands over the puppy, white and fluffy. It's probably a few months old, a mix of Husky or Eskimo dog and maybe a smaller breed like a terrier. It's terribly cute but frightened to death.

I make cooing sounds to the puppy before hiding it in my coat, keeping it warm. "Okay," I say to them. "Let's go."

I'm glad that Brigs told us about the dog earlier because when we are just steps from the house, the front door flings open, bringing Jessica, warmth and the smell of spices.

"Oh, Brigs!" she cries out and just as I thought he's swept into the house in a wave of fawning parents. But it's the perfect opportunity for me to slip upstairs without them noticing, even though I quickly take off my boots so I don't track snow in the house.

I head into the room where Brigs will be staying and look around. The layout of all the rooms are pretty much the same. I undo my coat and take out the pup, placing him on the bed.

He looks up at me with wide, heart-breaking eyes and I could nearly kiss my brother for saving this little fluffball.

First things are first though. I quickly head to the toilet across the hall and snatch up the newspapers from the magazine rack. Then I go about setting them all out on the other side of the bed furthest from the door, where you can't see if someone were to poke their head in. I grab several stacks of books from the bookshelf and make a make-shift fence with them, corralling the newspapers to the wall.

The puppy watches me from the bed the whole time. I pick him up and place him in, then go into my room to get a sweater that I don't care if it gets destroyed. I fold it up, head back to Brigs' room and place it in the corner of the pen, making a nice soft bed for the pup to sleep on.

"You stay there," I tell him gently, pointing at the pen. "I'll be back with some water."

I quickly make my way down the stairs as silently as possible, which isn't usually easy when you're as tall and heavy as me. But everyone is now back in the drawing room, talking to Brigs and I work fast, getting a small bowl of water, plus grabbing a small piece of roast from inside the oven. I run those back upstairs, pleased to see that the puppy hasn't knocked over the books. In fact, he's curled up on the sweater, getting up when he sees me. I give him the water and meat, then leave on the bedside lamp before turning off the lights.

When I come back downstairs, my face is flushed and I feel like I've been running a marathon. I take off my coat and scarf and finally saunter into the drawing room, taking my place beside Kayla on the couch.

She looks at me with questioning eyes so I can only smile and nod, patting her on the leg. As long as the dog doesn't start barking up a storm, we should be okay. I'm sure since it's Brigs who found the dog, if George did find out, maybe the dog would be allowed to stay. But I also think George would think it's my dog anyway with Brigs taking the fall, and we'd all be ousted.

Brigs continues talking to George about his up-coming teaching position but when he briefly meets my eye and raises his brow in question, I give him a wink. So far, so good.

The evening ends up being a rather pleasant one. Maybe everyone is feeling the power of the storm, the reverence of Christmas Eve, but George seems totally fo-cused on Brigs, which is great. He only makes one thoughtless blunder when he brings up if Brigs will ever date again. That obviously didn't go over well. Brigs clammed up and through those piercing eyes of his, I could tell he was being brought into his own dark place, so similar to mine.

But Kayla, dear, sweet, fucking amazing Kayla, had a way of easing the tension. She got up and even though everyone was full and lazy from the delicious roast that Jessica prepared, she put on 'Jingle Bell Rock" and invited Donald to dance with her. That was a smart move. Brigs was too lost and aching to do it and George would have turned her down. And there's nothing funny about dancing with me. But Donald, my quiet, nerdy adopted father? Dancing with my feisty girlfriend? Yes. Now that's funny.

They ended up dancing for a few songs and then Jessica pulled me up and the four of us danced away Christmas Eve, feeling like idiots, but happy that the family has remained intact for at least another day.

CHAPTER SEVEN

Kayla

"Merry Christmas, love," Lachlan murmurs in my ear.

I turn over in bed, practically rolling into him. While I'm completely lazy and maybe a bit sore from all the silly dancing we did last night, and tempted to keep sleeping, the fact that it's Christmas hits me with a jolt. It's the one day of the year where I actually can't sleep in and spring out of bed like a livewire. Same goes for anytime I visit Disneyland.

This Christmas is no exception. I kiss Lachlan quickly and then get out of bed, sliding on my merry pajama pants and a fuzzy red sweater. Another great thing about Christmas: permission to stay in your pajamas until dinner.

At least, in most homes it's like that. I look over at Lachlan as he pulls on his pair of thin black pajama pants and try not to drool over his bare torso.

"We don't have to dress up for Christmas morning, do we?" I ask.

"Don't be silly," he says, slipping on a white t-shirt. "We better go check on Brigs and the puppy, though."

Out in the hall, "Hark the Herald Angels Sing" and sounds of laughter waft up from downstairs, along with the smell of bacon and eggs. My stomach grumbles, despite the load of roast and Yorkshire pudding I had last night. You'd think I'd be too excited to eat, but I'm feeling ravenous about everything.

Lachlan knocks on Brigs' door.

"Just a minute," we hear him say.

"It's me," Lachlan says.

"Oh. Come in."

He opens the door and we step inside to see Brigs lying on his stomach on the bed, his long frame half hanging off. The puppy is in front of him, rolling on his back and chewing on one of Brigs' fingers.

Brigs looks up at us sheepishly. "He's a monster this little one. Cried all night until finally I had to bring him up into the bed with me. Course I couldn't sleep one bloody wink for fear of crushing the little bastard in the night."

"Well you look like you're suffering," Lachlan remarks, folding his arms across his chest. He peers over the side of the bed. "Though things are going to get right stinky in here if you don't clean that up."

Brigs eyes him pleadingly. "I thought maybe you could help. They'll be suspicious why I'm going outside."

Lachlan shakes his head. "No way. Your dog. Your shit. Those are the rules."

Brigs sighs and lays down his head, inviting the puppy to come pounce on it, paws first. It's too cute for words but I can tell Lachlan wants out of there before Brigs convinces him otherwise.

Downstairs we find everyone gathered around the kitchen table. Contrary to what Lachlan said, they're all dressed up. Okay, they're still in pajamas, but Donald looks like he's channeling Hugh Hefner and Jessica might as well be some old Hollywood star with her plush robe. George even looks dashing too, donning a striped, perfectly pressed set.

"You're up, good," Jessica says, gesturing to our place settings and pouring us juice. "Sit down. Where's Brigs?"

"He'll be down in a minute," Lachlan says. "Says he thought he lost a glove outside in the snow." Ah, such a good brother and so quick with the lies. And a few minutes later when we do see Brigs momentarily go outside with a plastic bag to go dispose of the newspapers somewhere in a snow bank (George is going to have a nice surprise when the snow melts – Merry Christmas old grump, here's some shit), the cover-up is solid.

"So Kayla," Donald says to me as Jessica dishes out the tattie scones, these wonderful triangles of potatoey goodness. "Are you ready to try haggis tonight?"

"I'll try anything once," I say just as Brigs sits down beside me.

"I'm sure you do," he says with a smirk and I kick him with my foot under the table. I have to admit, it's kind of nice to have this comradery with Brigs now, makes me feel more like I've been accepted into this family, especially on a day like today.

"Donald is in charge of the haggis," George says, taking a sip of his tea with shaky hands. "Best haggis in town."

"Ah," Donald says, looking bashful. He clears his throat. "Well, thank you, dad."

"Of course this town is full of sheep farmers and inbreds, so that's not saying much, now is it?"

Donald laughs and I jump to his defense. "I'm sure it will be great," I say.

"You say that now," Lachlan says. "You do know what it is and how it's made, aye? Puts black pudding to shame."

"Yes, I know what it's made of and I don't need a reminder."

"Well just so you know, I've made a vegetarian option as well," Jessica speaks up, sitting down and spreading her napkin on her lap. "It's very similar to the stuffing you Americans put in turkey on Thanksgiving."

"Sounds delicious, both of them." Wow. I should totally win points for diplomacy. I don't think I've ever been so agreeable at this time of the morning before.

When we're done with breakfast, we move out to the drawing room, taking our usual places.

"Kayla," Jessica says, holding out a Santa hat, "you're the youngest here, so we are passing on the McGregor family tradition for you to hand out all the presents."

"Ha," Lachlan laughs. "Sucker."

I glare at him but politely take the hat and put it on. It would be so much easier to just sit back and open presents but now I have a job to do. The funny thing is, my own family had this same tradition and growing up I was also the one who handed out the gifts.

I end up telling them all this as I search for presents under the massive tree. "We even celebrated Christmas until January 6th, which was great for getting rid of those post-Christmas blues."

"Why was that?" Donald asks.

I peer at a present that happens to be for him. "My father was Icelandic and that's just the tradition over there. Naturally me and my brothers wanted the extended Christmas festivities, even if we had more of the Japanese culture in our house."

I hand him the present. "For you." Then I move about to the next ones, purposely leaving my presents till the very end, as well as the ones I bought for people.

Everyone tears into everything. Well, Brigs and Lachlan do, while Jessica and Donald open theirs neatly. My mother used to do that too, saving the wrapping paper in a big pile. Every single year. And then when Christmas rolled around again, she'd forget and go out and buy more wrapping paper. When my brothers and I started going through all the stuff in the house a few months ago after her death, I found boxes and boxes of the used and so gently folded wrapping paper in the closet.

The thought of that causes my heart to contract painfully and I have to take in a sharp breath. But as I watch the McGregors holding up socks and dishware and candles and even underwear and thanking each other with big smiles on their faces, I have to remember that even though the memories of my family, my past, will hurt for a long time, I can still smile through the pain. I shouldn't be afraid to remember the good times, or the bad. I shouldn't be afraid to hurt because the pain only means that whatever I had with my parents was so very beautiful. I'm gutted, scooped out by the loss of my mother and yet somehow filled that she was such a wonderful driving force in my life. She made me who I am. She's the reason I'm here to begin with.

And now, now this is a family I may one day call my own. Even for just today, even though the grandfather is a crotchety old fart with no filter, I do feel accepted. I at least feel loved – beyond loved – by the man with the tattoos, the troubled man with the giant, endless heart. And that feeling is enough to carry me on through the day and onto all the next ones.

"Kayla, you haven't opened any of yours," Jessica says. She points at a large one wrapped in shiny silver paper. "Here, open that. That's from me, George, and Donald."

I sit down at the base of the tree and start unwrapping, putting on my game face in the event that it's something horrible and I still have to pretend to like it.

But it's not horrible at all. It's a bit generic, the kind of gift you probably would give the girlfriend of your son that you don't quite know all that well yet, but nice nonetheless. A fancy bath set with Scottish oatmeal soaps, loofahs, that sort of thing, along with a silk red robe and fluffy slippers.

I tell them all that I love it but then Jessica says there is something at the bottom. I look through the tissue and my fingers clench over something hard and worn. I pull it out to find a leatherbound notebook in my hands.

I look at her expectantly and she just smiles. "It's for your thoughts and your dreams. The journal has been in my family forever, never used, just always present. I fancied one day that someone would take a pen to it and write the next great novel, create a whole new world on the pages. I hope that someone can be you."

Honestly, my black soul swells like a sweet red balloon. A tear spills down my cheek as I look over at Lachlan who nods, smiling softly, as if telling me it's true, it's real, it's okay. I get up and go over and hug her, thanking her profusely for such a thoughtful gift. The bath stuff is great, but this came from the heart and I'm suddenly worried that my present won't measure up in the way I wanted it to.

And Lachlan gets up, picking up our joint gift and giving it to them. He then hands a present to George – one that I said I would go with Lachlan on, and then the framed picture to Brigs.

They open them in order. Jessica and Donald fawn over the Christmas ornaments while George gives an appreciative grunt to the set of Cuban cigars we picked up for him. But Brigs' reaction is the best. The minute he tears open the paper, his eyes widen and he bursts into loud, unabashed laughter.

"Where the hell did you get this?" Brigs asks between laughs, passing the picture around to Jessica and Donald.

"It was Kayla's idea," Lachlan says, nudging me.

I shrug. "I thought you could hang it up in your bathroom or something."

He grins at me, taking the picture back from his parents and staring it over, him in Buster Keaton form. "I would be honored to have a Buster Keaton version of myself staring at me while I take a shit."

"Brigs!" Jessica chastises him, but she's still laughing.

"All right, my turn, then Lachlan," Brigs says. "Of course Lachlan will naturally outdo me, the wanker." He gestures to a thin, square box under the tree.

I open it to find a rugby calendar from years ago with a half-naked man on the cover. Actually, the half-naked man is Thierry. I nearly jump out of my skin. There's the Frenchman, posing in a shower, with the photo barely cutting out his goods. I never thought I'd see Thierry like this but, *damn*.

"Oh my god, Brigs," Lachlan moans, covering up his face with his hands and falling back into the sofa.

My mouth drops as I slowly open it. "Is the infamous nude rugby calendar?"

"I'm so glad I can't see properly," George mutters to himself.

"Look at Mr. September," Brigs says happily while Lachlan lets out another embarrassed groan.

Making sure I don't flash his family with this calendar of cock and muscle, I carefully flip through the months until I come to September. Sure enough there is a side view of Lachlan on the rugby pitch, his firm ass on display, those giant quads of his looking extra menacing in the shadowy, grainy photograph.

Shit. And to think this is the man I love, the man I get to screw every day. I give myself an internal high five, like I have many times over the past few weeks.

"Wow," I say, closing it before things get weird. "I think I'll hang this in our bathroom too."

"Please don't," Lachlan whimpers, eventually taking his fingers away from his face. I think the man is blushing for a change.

"So, Lachlan," Brigs says, slapping his thighs. "Let's see what you can come up with."

We are the only two who haven't opened our presents from each other. For a moment my heart flutters, especially when I see his present under the tree, the only one left beside mine. It's a small box. Like, small enough for a ring. And of course that gets me thinking, both in fear and excitement. It can't be what I think it can…can it? So soon? Here? Now?

"Uh, why don't you open mine first," I tell Lachlan, throwing my package his way. It's light and he catches it with ease.

I had no clue what to get him so I figured the easiest thing would be to get something for the dogs. For better or for worse, he loves those dogs more than he loves himself. So I went out and had three dog sweaters made with their names on them. I've heard him say a few times that they could use them when it's snowing like it is and it just stuck in my head. Plus, how cute would they all look, walking together in matching outfits? No one could be scared of them then, even with muzzles.

Lachlan seems speechless as he holds up Lionel's, Emily's and Jo's cable-knit sweaters, all with their names knitted in contrasting yarn.

"I'm not sure if they'll fit," I try and explain. "It was hard trying to measure Emily, she nearly took my head off."

"They'll fit," he says, almost whispering, as he runs his fingers over them. He looks to me, his beautiful eyes burning into mine, trying to tell me all that his lips cannot.

I kiss him on the cheek and he relaxes himself against me, pulling me into a hug. "Thank you," he says quietly. "This means so much."

I run my fingers along his strong jaw and smile, careful not to get too carried away with a captive audience.

"Only one more gift Kayla," Jessica says, clearing her throat. I pull away from Lachlan's warmth and look at her shining face. Even she seems a bit emotional over the sweater situation.

I nod and pick it up from under the tree. As I slowly unwrap the plain brown packaging, I try not to let my thoughts run away on me. Runaway thoughts have never done me any good.

But, when the packaging peels away, I'm left with a jewelry box and it's hard not to think about it. What if it's an engagement ring? What would I say? Isn't it too soon? Would Lachlan really take such a private moment and share it with his family, with his grandfather?

"Just open it," Brigs says.

I do.

I gasp.

It's not an engagement ring at all. In fact, it's almost better.

I carefully reach in and hold up a silver necklace, a locket in shape of a heart, engraved with delicate flowers and stars across the face. It shines brightly, probably the prettiest piece of jewelry I've ever had. I look up to see Lachlan staring at me expectantly so I look for the snap on the side of the locket and pry it open.

On one side there is a picture of us together. Very small, just our smiling faces, but in black and white. I think it was taken at the Ruff Love gala over the summer. On the other side it says something in what I think is Gaelic. Something I can't pronounce properly. *Sibhe mo clann.*

"It's beautiful," I tell him breathlessly. "What does it say?"

"It says, you are my clan."

Jessica makes a dreamy sigh.

I feel like my insides are dancing, my heart buzzing, my blood fizzing like champagne.

"I'm your clan," I repeat, my pulse racing loudly.

"Aye," he says. "That and more."

I swallow hard, those pesky tears finding me again. I want to take him upstairs and show him what this gift, this beautiful, thoughtful, emotional gift means to me. But I can't. Not here. Not now. All I can do is hug him, kiss him and hope he knows that he's my clan too, always and forever.

I feel like I'm walking on a cloud for the rest of the day. Even when we go outside to help Brigs dispose of more puppy poo and walk up the lane to check on Brigs' car and to see if the neighbors are home yet (they aren't), the cold doesn't bother me a bit. My heart is a glowing furnace, keeping me warm, and the necklace rests against my chest like it's always been there.

***

When the darkness starts to fall, bathing the house in twilight, I gather with Brigs in his room with Lachlan and the puppy. Christmas dinner is almost ready, the house smells absolutely amazing, and I'm gearing up to finally try haggis.

We're also playing with the puppy, whom Brigs has already named "Winter." I called my brothers back home earlier to wish them a merry Christmas, and while it was so good to hear their voices, it also cut deep to not be with them. But puppies are a quick fix to pain.

"You can't give the dog a name if you aren't going to keep it," Lachlan tells Brigs.

"Sure I can," Brigs says as he sits his tall frame on the edge of the bed. "You name your shelter dogs all the time. Besides, if it turns out it's not the neighbor's dog, then you're keeping it, not me."

"What?" Lachlan says as the little fluffball plays with leftover wrapping paper. "The shelter is no place for a dog that young. He needs a home. Training. Complete love."

"You need to take him," I tell Brigs. "The little guy already looks up to you. He thinks you're dad. You just named him for crying out loud."

Brigs shrugs. "I'll try again in the morning. Then I have to leave and the dog isn't coming with me."

"Well aren't you just a puppy Scrooge," I tell him.

He doesn't seem that phased though I can tell from the way he's playing with Winter, that he's far more attached to the white pup than he pretends. I just hope by the time the holiday is over, Winter is reunited with his family or Brigs comes to his senses.

Eventually we make our way downstairs ready for the feast. The kitchen table is prepped with silver candle-sticks, elegant cutlery and a range of steaming dishes all laid out on a pristine white tablecloth with red trim. In the middle is a beautiful centerpiece of pine cones, ribbon, holly and fir that I have a hunch Jessica made and arranged herself. She's a regular old Martha Stewart this one.

We take our seats, Lachlan and I beside each other with George at one end of the table and Brigs at the other. While I'm just wearing a simple black dress and maroon cardigan, my necklace the star of the look, everyone else looks done up. Even Lachlan is wearing a white shirt with no tie, unbuttoned just enough to show a hint of his tattoos.

Jessica leads us into a quick prayer and then it's time to eat.

I've just dolloped out a scoop of mashed potatoes and am thinking about the haggis, which really does look like a type of stuffing, when George says, "Where the hell is the wine? Not even sherry?"

Jessica gives him a placating smile. "We have sparkling apple juice or the mulled wine from IKEA."

"There's no alcohol in those," he says. "You can't have Christmas without wine. This is ridiculous."

Donald gets up and grabs George's glass. "Let me get you some of the sherry, dad," he says.

"Get me some? Bring the bottle here. There's two bottles of red in the cupboard by the sherry, bring those too." He eyes Jessica. "I don't want to take from my own collection, but I will if I have to. It's Christmas, for Christ's sake. Yes, his literal sake."

I flinch while Lachlan has grown still beside me, holding his breath and avoiding eye contact.

I put my hand on his arm. "Are you okay?" I whisper.

He nods. "I'm fine. Really." He attempts to smile but the pain in his eyes betrays it.

I believe him too, that he will be fine, until Donald comes back with the wine and George insists he pour some for everyone.

"None for me," Lachlan says quickly, covering his glass.

"Me neither," I add. "But thank you though."

George narrows his eyes at us. "No wine? Lachlan, you were usually the first one to finish the bottle. What's wrong with you?"

"Nothing is wrong with him, grandpa," Brigs says but offers no more than that. None of us want to be the one to say it, if we even have to say it at all.

"Well something is," he says. "I haven't seen him for a year. Suddenly he's stopped drinking and has some half Chinese girlfriend. I don't even know you anymore, do I Lachlan. Perhaps I never did," he adds under his breath. "You Lockharts are a strange breed, not like us McGregors."

You can cut the tension above the table with a carving knife. I can see what it comes down to, even now. While Lachlan considers me part of his clan, George doesn't consider Lachlan to be part of his. I don't think it matters what Lachlan says or does, if he was a rugby player or a politician, an alcoholic or a church-going saint – in his eyes, he's not one of them.

Lachlan clears his throat and stares at George dead in the eye. "No. I'm not really a McGregor am I? But I am here, just as I always have been. I have your last name. I have this family's heart, as well as my own. I would just hope that one day, just as I said to Kayla, that you could see I consider you my clan and maybe one day, you'll consider me to be yours."

The room falls silent.

"Still doesn't explain why you're not drinking," George mutters, cutting into the turkey on his plate.

"Because I'm an alcoholic," Lachlan says, so matter-of-factly I nearly spit out my water. "I've always been one and always will be one. My whole life I've dealt with my problems, my past, my own soul, by using drugs or drinking my way out of it. You can only get away with it for so long and it wasn't until I met Kayla, that I opened up my own eyes to what I was putting her through. What I was putting my family through. What I was putting myself through. You can judge me all you want, blame my clan, my origins, blame me for being a black sheep. But the truth is the truth and while I may not wear it proudly, it is mine."

Everyone seems to hold their breath, waiting for George's reaction. But I'm not holding my breath – I can barely breathe. This man…just when I thought he couldn't surprise me anymore, he just laid his heart out on the table and all the ugliness that comes with it, for all the world to see. He expects to be hurt, to be ridiculed, to be judged and he still did it anyway. He did it because that's him. He's Lachlan McGregor, Lachlan Lockhart, my beast and the bravest man I've ever known.

The amount of love I have for him exceeds the deepest reaches of anything.

Infinite and uncontained.

Tested.

True.

Finally George clears his throat, making everyone jump slightly in their seats.

"So you can't handle your liquor," he says in his gruff brogue. "Maybe you are a McGregor after all."

The joke is barely funny. But it's a joke. And maybe the closest thing Lachlan will ever get to being accepted. Everyone bursts out into laughter, nervous at first, then one filled with relief. I can only squeeze Lachlan's arm, right over his tattoo of Lionel the Lion, and stare at him like the googly-eyed lovebird that I am.

And, after that, everything seems fine. The tension dissipates. George has his sherry, Donald has a glass of wine, while the rest of us do it up with sparkling apple juice, sipping it like fine champagne. There is a sense of rightness, of peace, and the falling snow outside the windows just adds to the magical feeling of Christmas.

That is until we hear a loud CRASH from the drawing room. We all freeze, exchanging glances, then jump to our feet, filing out down the hall and into the drawing room.

The tree is completely knocked over, sprawled over the couch, ornaments and tinsel everywhere.

"How did this happen?" Donald exclaims as we gingerly come over.

Suddenly, at the base of the tree, a pile of the used wrapping paper starts moving.

"Oh my goodness," Jessica says, hand to her chest, nearly clutching her actual pearls. "What is it, a rat?"

"Has anyone ever seen National Lampoons Christmas Vacation?" I ask absently, thinking it could be a squirrel or perhaps someone wrapped a cat.

But then the wrapping paper shakes some more.

Small, pointed puppy ears poke out and then the rest of Winter's white head.

"The little bugger!" Brigs says while Jessica cries out, "Oh my god, is that a dog?" She looks to Lachlan. "Is that yours?"

"Actually it's Brigs'," Lachlan says while Brigs crouches down and approaches the puppy, scooping him up into his arms before he can run away.

"Brigs," George says sternly. "You know how I feel about animals."

Brigs sighs, cradling Winter to him. From the way the puppy looks at everyone in the room, mild fear, strong curiosity, it's impossible not to fall in love with the pup. "We all know, grandpa, but I found him in the barn, the farm next door, and there was no one around. I wasn't about to let it starve and freeze to death. We even went by earlier to see if there was anyone home, but they're gone."

"They always go away on Christmas," George says, eyeing the puppy. He looks up at Brigs and squints, making some internal decision. "The dog can stay. But if he shits anywhere, it's your problem. Tomorrow we'll bring him back where he belongs. Just so you know though...I'll be watching you."

As if on cue, Winter looks at George and sticks out his tongue.

Christmas rolls to a merry end.

CHAPTER EIGHT

Lachlan

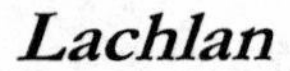

It's late when Kayla and I finally retire to bed. Jessica and Donald are down by the fire, Jessica drinking the sherry she didn't dare drink in front of me earlier, talking and listening to the last of the Christmas music. I know we will still have Christmas music going tomorrow on Boxing Day, but Christmas day feels different from all the rest. It's the last time it counts.

Brigs is in his room with the dog, probably grappling with saying goodbye in the morning, while I think George fell asleep in his recliner.

Aside from the faint strain of the music, the house is silent. The snow has stopped falling, adding to the hush.

And Kayla, beautiful Kayla, is staring at me with so much love, my heart can hardly take it.

"Lachlan," she says, pressing her naked body against me and I close my eyes at the feel of her sweet warmth against my skin.

"Yes, love?"

"I want to work for you," she whispers.

"What?" I pause, thinking she must be joking. "Are you taking the piss?"

"No," she says quickly. "Not in the slightest. I want to help you, help Ruff Love. I think you're right. I'd be really good at it."

I twist around so I'm facing her, her skin lit up from the blue of moonlit snow. "Why the change of heart?"

She traces her fingers over my tattoos, staring at them intently. "Because. I want to help. I want to be a part of everything to do with you." She looks up, eyes glistening. "I love you. So much. And I know you're trying to help me but you're also asking me to be a part of something big and meaningful. I want that. If you're helping me, I want to help you."

I'm so moved by this but also afraid. "I don't want you to feel pressured into this at all. I just want you to be happy."

"I am happy," she says emphatically. "With you. Lachlan…tonight. Fuck, every night. Every day. You continue to surprise me. You make me fall in love, deeper and deeper, enough so that when I went back home, through all the shit that happened, it was thoughts of you that kept me going. The chance that maybe I'd see you again. I don't want to fuck any of that up. I want to be with you for as long as I can and if working at Ruff Love can help that become a reality, well that's a reality I want."

"And your writing…"

"My writing will always be there. I'll keep trying on the side. But until it happens, this is where I want to be."

"You have no idea how happy you've just made me," I tell her, my voice becoming choked. I bring her into me, kissing the top of her head, then down her face, absolutely consumed by my feelings for her. They flicker, deep flames, and I have no desire to ever put them out.

I only want to fan them until they take us both.

I move back on the bed, taking my lips from her cheek, to her mouth, to her collarbone and all the way down the middle of her body. She slowly squirms underneath me in languid anticipation.

I lick a line down each hipbone and then bury my face between her legs. Her smell makes me harder than a rock, wanting so desperately to be inside of her but first I indulge my tongue, wanting to give, give, give. It's only been a few days but that's a few days too long.

Kayla tastes so unbelievably good, addictive as always, and I groan into her, the vibrations making her moan. My tongue swirls around her clit before plunging inside of her.

She's wet as sin and growing slicker by the moment, hips grinding into my face. Greedy, greedy girl. Just the way I love her.

Then her hands are in my hair, a tight fist, and her legs are splayed wider, needing more. I pull back, wanting to be a tease and gently blow on her cunt until she's begging for it.

I attack her with my tongue, pulsing it in and out of her. She's so silky, so tight, and soon she's coming as I press my tongue over her clit, her thighs wrapped on either side of my head and squeezing tight, her skin throbbing beneath my lips. She manages to keep from being as loud as she usually is but her low moans are deadly.

I can't help but look up. She's gripping the sheets for dear life, her back arched and her perfect mouth open. Any other night I'd think she was begging for my cock, but tonight I want to be as deep inside of her as possible. I need, crave, our connection.

I get between her legs, and, grabbing her thighs, pull her back toward me, keeping her legs up. I position myself at her entrance, so wet and ready, like a second home. My only home.

"God, you're beautiful," I manage to whisper. I clench my jaw and stare down at her as I slowly push my cock in. She's still breathing heavily, her head rolling back and forth on the pillow, her dark hair splayed beneath her.

I stare down at my cock where I ease into her, her legs in my hands, my ass driving me in deep, deep, deep. I lift up her legs higher, my fingers digging into her flesh, and thrust in at a sharper angle. I know I'm hitting her G-spot when she groans and starts gripping the sheets again.

She looks up at me briefly with shiny eyes and wild bed-head, biting her lip. I know it's the look that I'm doing something brilliant to her. It's the look I always chase.

I push in again, slowly dragging myself out so I'm hitting all the right nerves. She's always so tight, that beautiful fist around me.

She gasps as her nerves erupt, her eyes pinching shut, her mouth falling open again. And I want more of it. I want to blow her bloody mind.

I reach down and start petting her clit with hard, quick little taps that happen in time with my thrusts as my hips piston myself in and out of her. In and out. With each slow, deliberate push, I feel her become undone around me. She's squirming underneath me and I know she's praying to come, for that release. The pressure from my fingers and my cock is just too much for her to handle and every second of this torture is all mine.

We slowly build to a crescendo. And as much as I want to go fast, we go as if we have all the time in the world. We move together, as one, sweat on sweat, skin on skin, heart to heart.

Kayla comes first, as she usually does, as she always should. Her eyes widen as if in shock, as if the orgasm has a real grip and is pulling her somewhere, taking her by surprise. But where she's being taken, it has to be heaven.

She cries out, loud for a moment before I manage to briefly press my palm against her mouth to gently stifle her. I can feel her hot breath, her wet lips, her moans as they try to escape. Her cheeks flush, chest rises and her eyes can barely focus. She's flying high.

And she's flying with me. I come just as intensely, my cum slamming inside of her, hot and fast, as she squeezes me, the orgasm ripping through both of us. I moan, taking my hand away from her mouth, feeling powerless against everything except the sunshine rising deep inside me, blasting away the night, the dark, the unknown.

The shadows are gone.

I am here.

I am there.

I am hers.

Completely.

When we've both caught our breaths, we curl up into each other and I pull the covers over us, tucking us in tight.

Christmas may be over.

But we have just begun.

***

Breakfast the next morning is somewhat melancholic. It's a strange feeling, to actually feel part of a family, something deep and organic. I know I've felt it over the years, but when you're an orphan, that longing, that search to belong, it never really leaves you. But at least now, after last night, it's abated. There is peace. There is relief. And when it's all over, I think I'll be just a wee bit sad.

"Well, I guess it's time I go check in with the neighbors," Brigs says, downing a glass of orange juice before getting up.

"I'll go with you," I offer and he nods. Kayla is busy helping Jessica clean up, so it's just us brothers.

We bundle up and then head out into the snow, Winter kept hidden and warm in Brigs' coat. After the dark storm for the last few days, the sunshine and snow is blinding.

We don't talk about much as we walk. Brigs doesn't seem to want to discuss London and the teaching position, so I steer the conversation into film, something that animates him.

But he turns it to Kayla.

"I really thought you were going to propose to her," Brigs says.

I give him a steady look. "It's not the right time."

"Will there be a right time?"

"Why are you so curious?"

"Guess I just want you to be happy," Brigs says with a shrug. "Besides, I like her. She's a ballbuster and she's good for you. Dare I say you might be good for her."

I sigh. I have to admit, it feels good to hear it from him. "Things will happen in due time. For now though, I'm just happy she's here. That she's staying."

"And the job hunt?"

"She's working for me now," I tell him.

"You old dog," he says, grinning. "Getting your girlfriend to work for you."

"I'll be paying her," I remind him.

"Yeah. Just don't get that all confused as to what you're paying for."

"Shut it, Brigs."

It's not long before we end up at the neighbors and Brig's car, half-buried in the snow. It's going to take a team of us later on to dig him out but it at least looks like the neighbors are home now.

We knock on the door and Brigs brings Winter out of his coat. The little pup wriggles around, trying to lick Brigs' face and in that moment, I see that Brigs is going to have a hard time giving him up if he has to. I hate to admit it, but that makes me happy. Now he knows. Now he gets it. It's hard to let go of man's best friend.

Mrs. MacAuley, a middle-aged lady with salt and pepper Hilary Clinton hair, answers the door. I recognize her and she recognizes us.

"The McGregor boys," she says. "Merry Christmas to you."

"Merry Christmas," we say in unison, like a bunch of stupid kids.

"Listen," Brigs says, as her eyes focus on the puppy. "I drove my car into a snowbank just over there the other night. No one here was home and I ended up in the barn, looking. I came across this little puppy all alone so I took him in so he wouldn't die in the cold. We were wondering if it belonged to you."

She shakes her head. "My heavens. What an angel he is," she says, touching the tip of his coal-black nose. "But he's not ours. I've never seen him before."

"You're sure?" Brigs asks.

She nods. "Absolutely."

"And you don't want him?" I ask her and I can feel Brigs' icy eyes on me.

"Oh, goodness, no. I love dogs but Allistair is allergic. Surely you can find a home though. You still run that shelter, don't you Lachlan?"

"Aye," I tell her. "We'll find a loving home. Just wanted to make sure."

We thank her for her time, wish her a happy new year, and then walk back to the house, the snow crunching beneath our boots.

"I can't believe you offered her the dog," Brigs say to me as an aside.

"Well, you said you didn't want the dog," I tell him, my voice light. I breathe in and out the fresh air, my breath hanging in a frosted cloud. "Unless you do."

Brigs doesn't say anything.

I clear my throat. "Look, I get it. I do. They're a lot of responsibility."

"That's not it," he says darkly.

"I'm not done. They're a lot of responsibility. A lot of time, commitment and care. But most of all, they're about a lot of love. It's about opening yourself up and experiencing something unconditional while trying to give it in return. Because lord knows, dogs will test that love and patience every time they chew your favorite shoe or piss in your bed."

"Lachlan, you don't have to do your spiritual dog spiel on me."

I continue. "The thing is, loving something after you've lost so much is scary. I know this and yet I can't even pretend to know it the way that you do. Loving a dog, letting it into your life. It's like letting in love. Falling in love. It's about getting attached to something that will die in your lifetime. And it's horrible to think that way but I think that's why we get so attached to animals, to our pets. We outlive them. Their time on earth is limited and they have nothing but love to give. But that's what makes every day with them even sweeter. Loving a dog is about loving and losing. But your heart comes out bigger, and stronger, in the end."

Brigs is silent for a few moments, the only sound is our breath and our footsteps along the road, everything else muffled by the snow.

Finally he says, "Shit, Lachlan. Why don't you put that on your Ruff Love brochures?"

"Only if it works with you."

When we get inside the house, everyone is gathered by the fireplace for one last cup of tea. Kayla is surrounded by Tupperware containers filled with turkey and haggis (the vegetarian kind – the original didn't sit too well with her).

"How did it go?" Jessica asks.

"I see you still have the mutt," George comments bitterly.

"It's not theirs," I tell them. "They've never seen the puppy before."

"So I guess he's going to Ruff Love then," Jessica says sadly.

I'm about to nod when Brigs says, "Actually, he's staying with me." I grin as Brigs raises the white snowball in the air. "Everyone, say hello to Winter McGregor."

Everyone, minus George, says a cheery greeting, with Jessica and Kayla getting up to coo at the puppy. I clap Brigs joyfully on the back before I grab Kayla by the arm and pull her to me, kissing her forehead.

I look at everyone around me.

So many of us beaten up by life.

But still here.

Still breathing.

My people.

My heart.

My clan.

The End

Thank you for reading Winter Wishes. After this, you may want to read the epilogue to The Play again, as it takes place after this novella and really cements Kayla and Lachlan's relationship.

For an exclusive sneak peek at the first two chapters of The Lie, releasing Feb 15th, read on…

The Lie
New York Times and USA Today Bestselling Author
KARINA HALLE

The Lie

By Karina Halle

PROLOGUE

Brigs

Four years ago

"I'm sorry."

I'd rehearsed it so many times that I thought I could just open my mouth and the words would flow out. The whole speech. The entire confession. I thought if I kept saying it over and over again in my head, that when it came time to speak the awful, horrible, liberating truth, that it would come easily.

But it doesn't. It hasn't.

I can't even explain myself. All I do is drop to both my knees, my legs shaking from the stress of it all, the stress I brought upon myself, that pales in comparison to what she's about to feel.

Miranda is sitting on the couch, like I'd asked her to, the cup of tea placed neatly on the saucer. I keep my eyes focused on the subtle wafts of steam rising from it. I thought I could do the right thing and meet her eyes but I can't. I'm cowardly at the end of it all, unwilling to see the pain, the deep cuts at my own hand.

"Sorry for what?" she asks in that calm voice of hers. Always so calm, able to weather any storm I've thrown her way. The fact that I'm on my knees, visibly trembling like a fool, hasn't changed her tone in the slightest. Maybe this won't be as hard on her as I thought.

Bloody wishful thinking that is.

I take in a deep breath and wince when it comes out shaking. I wish the sound of the rain pouring outside would mask it.

"I'm sorry," I repeat again. My voice sounds hollow, like I'm hearing a playback of it on a dusty old tape. "I have to tell you something."

"I can see that," she says and now I detect an edge. "You asked me to sit down and now you're on your knees. I hope you're not proposing to me all over again."

It would all be so much easier if that were true.

I finally dare to meet her eyes.

My wife is such a beautiful woman. Grace Kelly reincarnated. A neck like a swan. I remember our first date. We'd barely been out of high school but even then it's like she held a world of secrets in her poise. She was so put together, so perfect. I showed up with my shitty car and took her to the movies and dinner at the best place I could afford, even though the food was bloody horrible. And she was forever gracious, didn't bat an eye. She made me feel like I was somebody when I was with her and maybe that's why I married her. She was everything I wasn't.

She's still everything I'm not. That can't be more apparent than now.

"Brigs," she says, frowning. She barely has lines even when she's making that face. "You're scaring me."

I clear my throat but it's like pushing boulders. "I know."

"Is it about Hamish?" she asks and as that thought comes over her, her eyes widen in panic.

I shake my head quickly. "No, nothing to do with Hamish."

I'm thankful more than ever that the little man has gone to bed when he's supposed to. The rain is coming down harder now, tapping at the windows, and that has always worked on him better than any lullaby.

"I just want you to know," I tell her, putting my palm on her hands. So soft, like she never worked a day in her life. I used to make fun of her for that, for being the socialite, the trust-fund baby. Right now they make her seem achingly vulnerable. "I just want you to know that...I've put a lot of thought into this. I never wanted to hurt you." I stare at her, begging with my eyes. "You must know that."

"Oh god," she says with a gasp, bringing her hand away from mine. "Brigs, what did you do?"

The weight of all my choices blankets me.

There is no easy way to say this.

No way to soften the blow.

I don't want to hurt her.

But I have to.

"I..." I swallow the razors in my throat. I shake my head and fight the heat behind my eyes. "Miranda, I want a divorce."

She stares at me blankly, so calmly, I wonder if she's heard me. My hands are shaking, my heart is about to need resuscitation. "What?" she finally whispers in obvious disbelief.

To outside eyes we've had a happy marriage. But we both knew this was coming. Maybe she never saw the catalyst, but she knew this was coming. She had to know.

"We've both been very unhappy for a long time," I explain.

"Are you serious?" she says quickly. "Are you seriously doing this?"

"Miranda." I lick my lips, daring to meet her eyes. "You must have known this was going to happen. If it wasn't from me, it would have been from you."

"How dare you," she says, roughly pushing my hands away and getting to her feet. "How dare you put words in my mouth? I've been happy…I've just been…I've just been…"

She's shaking her head violently, walking to the other side of the living room. "No," she says, standing against the mantle. "No, I won't give you a divorce. I won't let you leave. You can't leave me. You…You Brigs McGregor could never leave Miranda Harding McGregor. You would be nothing without me."

I let her words deflect, even though my belief in them is what's led to this moment. "Miranda," I say softly, and her name is starting to sound foreign, the way it can when you say a word too many times in a row. "Please."

"No!" she yells and I flinch, hoping she doesn't wake up Hamish. "Whatever foolish ideas are coming over your brain, I don't know, but a divorce isn't the answer. This is just...this just flights of fancy for you. This you being unhappy at your job. This is you not feeling like a man. This is you not performing like a man."

A dig below the literal belt. I should have known that would be her first line of defense. Our problems in the bedroom for the last year. I can't fault her for that.

"No," she says again. "I can live with that, I can. And if I never have another child, so be it. But my family...my honor...it will not come to this. We have a good life, Brigs. This house. Look at this house." She points wildly around the room, a feverish look in her eyes. "Look at these things. We have everything. People look up to us. They envy us. Why would you throw that away?"

My heart sinks further down my chest, to my stomach, and burns there.

"Please," I say softly, not wanting the whole truth to come out but ready to wield it if I have to. "I'm not...I don't want to hurt you. But I'm just not in love with you anymore. It's the honest truth and I'm sorry, I'm so sorry."

She blinks, like she's been slapped. Then says, "So? What married couples *are* in love with each other? Be realistic here Brigs."

Now I'm surprised. I frown. I didn't expect her to fight for us so much. And to fight for a marriage she's okay with being loveless.

She's watching me closely, tapping her nails against her lips, plotting. The rain spatters at the windows and in the distance, thunder rumbles, the first autumn storm. The room seems smaller than ever.

"We can work it out," she finally says, her voice back to being eerily calm. "This is just a hiccup. We can work it out. You can love me again and if you can't, then it's okay. It's fine. No one has to know. We both love our son, that's enough. Don't you want him to grow up with a father, a complete family? Don't you know a divorce would destroy him? Is that what you want for him?"

I take an icepick to the chest with that one, the cold spreading through me. Because of course, *of course*, that's what I want for him. It's what's held me back and back and back. But kids know, they know when their parents aren't happy. Hamish deserves better than a childhood tainted with angst.

"Separated parents are better than two miserable parents together," I tell her, pleading now. "You know it's true. Hamish is smart, *so* smart, so intuitive. Children pick up on so much more than you realize."

Her eyes narrow. "Oh what self-help book did you steal that from? Bloody hell Brigs, just listen to yourself, talking out of your arse."

"Do you want him to grow up in a house where I don't love his mother? Is that what you want? Don't you think he'll see, he'll know."

"He won't," she says viciously. "Stop making excuses."

I get to my feet and raise my palms, feeling helpless to the core. Guilty as sin. "I have no excuses. Just the truth."

"Go fuck your truth, Brigs," she snaps.

The thunder crashes again. I pray it drowns out our argument, that Hamish is still blissfully asleep, unaware that his future is changing. Not for the worse, please God, not for the worse. Just changing.

She walks over the antique bar cart and pours herself a glass of Scotch from the decanter, like a heroine in a Hitchcock film, playing the part.

Can't she see how tired I am of pretending?

Doesn't she get tired too?

"Do you want one?" she asks over her shoulder, almost coyly, the glass between her manicured fingertips. Her father gave us those, and the decanter, as a wedding present.

I shake my head, trying to steady my heart.

She slams back the Scotch and in a second it's down her throat. "Suit yourself. I'll have your share."

She pours another glass, holds it delicately, and glides over to the couch, sitting down in front of me. She crosses her legs and stares up at me, cocking her head, a wave of straw blonde falling across her forehead. She's buried her emotions again, pretending, acting, as if that will make everything right.

"You're a fool, Brigs. Always were. But I forgive you. We all have lapses in judgement sometimes."

I sigh heavily and close my eyes. She's not getting it.

"People fall out of love all the time," she goes on, finishing half the glass and putting it down on the side table. The *clink* sounds so loud in this room that seems to be growing emptier and emptier. "It's a fact of life. A sad, sad fact. But you can fall back in. I'll try harder. I really will. I'll do anything to make you stay. You know this.

You know how I can be. Once I have something, I don't let go. I fight. And I keep what's mine."

I do know that. Which is why I have to give her the truth. The terrible truth. Because only then she'll see. Only then she'll see what I mean.

I wish I didn't have to do this.

"I'm so sorry," I whisper.

"I forgive you." She finishes the rest of her drink, wiping the back of her hand across her lips without managing to smear her lipstick.

"I'm so sorry," I say again, feeling the tears building behind my eyes. I shake my head sharply. "The truth is…I'm in love with someone else. I've fallen in love with someone else."

There.

The truth falls.

Lands on her like bricks.

She jerks her head back from the impact, eyes widening in confusion. Fear. Anger.

"What?!" she exclaims. She stares at me, the fury slowly building and building and building before it's unleashed. "Who? Who, tell me fucking who?!"

"It doesn't matter," I say but she's up on her feet, sneering at me, face red and contorted. Unable to pretend anymore.

"Tell me!" she screams, holding onto her head, her teeth bared, her eyes wild. "Tell me! Is it someone I know? Susan? Carol!?"

"It's no one you know, Miranda, it just happened, I-"

"Fuck you!" she screams again.

"Please, Hamish is sleeping-"

"Oh fuck you!" she pounds her fists against my chest and pushes me back. "Fuck you for making me the fool. What is she, some young tart, did she make you get it up? Huh, did she fix your problem?"

"I never slept with her," I tell her quickly.

"Oh bullshit!" she screams. "Bloody fucking hell. Brigs. Brigs you can't be serious. You're in love with someone else." She shakes her head, talking to herself. "You of all people. The professor. Quiet Mr. McGregor. No. I can't believe it. I can't fucking believe it."

"I know it's hard to hear."

Crack.

She slaps me hard.

Again.

And again.

One side and the other and I turn the cheek because I deserve this and I knew this was coming and if she didn't react this way, then I really didn't know the woman I married.

"You arse! You wanker!" She shoves me one more time and runs across the room, to the bar. She picks up the decanter of Scotch, downs a few gulps of it straight out of the nose, then spits some of it up, bent over in a coughing fit.

"Miranda please."

"You are disgusting!" she screeches after she's caught her breath. "Pathetic little shit! You slept with another woman, you –"

"I didn't!" I yell, my arms flying out to the sides. "I never slept with her, please believe that."

"And even if I believed you, you think that gives you a pass?" She nearly spits the words. "Love is a choice Brigs and you chose this. You chose to not love me and you chose to love her, some fucking whore. Some nobody. You chose to ruin our fucking lives!" At the last word she picks up the decanter of Scotch and hurls it at me. I duck just in time as it crashes against the cabinet behind me, breaking into a million pieces.

"Mummy?" Hamish whimpers, rubbing his eyes and standing in the doorway.

Fuck!

I whirl around, trying to smile. "Mummy is fine," I tell him. "Go back to sleep, buddy."

"Is it storming out?" he says, walking forward toward the broken glass.

"Hamish!" I yell at him, hands out for him to stop. He does before he reaches the glass, blinking at me – I never raise my voice around him. But before I can scoop him up, Miranda is running across the room and grabbing him by the arm.

"Come on baby, we're going, we're going," she says, taking him out of the living room and into the foyer.

I run after them in time to see Miranda grabbing her car keys and her coat. Hamish is crying now and she's picking him up in her arms.

"What are you doing?" I cry out, coming after her.

She quickly runs out the door and into the rain and I'm right behind her, bare feet sinking into cold mud, nearly slipping as she heads for the sedan.

She can't be serious. She can't do this.

I manage to grab hold of her arm as she puts Hamish in the front seat, closing the door. The car seat isn't even there, it's in the house, the maid was cleaning it after Hamish spilled his milk this afternoon.

"You can't take him!" I scream at her over the wind and rain.

"Let go of me!" she yelps, trying to pull away. "I'm taking him from you, you bastard."

"No, listen to me!" I tighten my grip on her arm. Hamish is wailing from inside the car, rain sliding down the window. "You're not thinking, you've had the Scotch. It's a fucking storm out there and he needs his car seat, just listen to me!"

"If you don't let go of me," she seethes, "I'm going to tell everyone that you hurt me and you'll never see your son again." She pulls against me harder, to make a point, my fingers automatically digging into her soft skin. "You can have your divorce, Brigs. But you can't have him."

"Miranda, please, let me get the car seat. Okay, I know you're angry but please, let me do that! Just let me do that." We are both soaked to the bone now and my feet are slowly being buried by mud. I'm feeling buried by my own desperation. "Please, okay please."

She stares at me, so fearful, so enraged. Then she nods, the rains spilling down her face.

I don't have a plan. But I know I'm not letting her drive away from here, not in her state of hysterics, not in this weather. I look down at Hamish as he's crying, his face pink in the dim light, nearly obscured by the rain.

"Just give me a second," I tell him, "Daddy will be right back."

I turn, running toward the house, wondering if I need to call the cops, if she'll calm down in the time I get the seat, if –

The car door slams.

I stop and whirl around.

She's running around the hood and getting in her side.

"No!" I scream. I try to run but slip, falling onto the ground. "Miranda, wait!"

The car starts just as I'm getting to my feet and I don't feel the cold or the rain or hear the wind or the engine, I just feel horror. Pure, unfiltered, unsaturated horror.

The front wheels spin viciously for a moment before it reverses back down the driveway.

I get to my feet as fast as I can which isn't fast enough and start running after her.

I reach the car, slam my hands down on the hood, staring at her through the moving wiper blades. Her face. Her indignity. Her panic. Her disgrace.

His face. Distraught. Confused. The perfect marriage of both of us. The perfect little boy.

Her face. His face.

The wipers wipe them clean.

She puts it in forward and guns the car, enough to push the grill into my hips and I quickly leap to the right before I get run over.

I roll over on the ground and struggle to my feet as Miranda whirls the car around and speeds off down the driveway.

"Miranda!" I scream, holding my head. Panic grips me for one second, freezing me in place, helpless, hopeless.

But I'm not.

I have to go after them.

I run back to the house, grab my mobile and the car keys to the vintage Aston Martin and run back out, jumping in the car.

The fucking old car takes a few times to roll over and I'm looking at the phone wondering if I should call the police. I don't even know if she's legally drunk or not and I don't want to get her in trouble either but if they can stop her before I can, before she possibly hurts herself and Hamish, then I may just have to. I have to do something.

I know she's heading to her parents, the Hardings, across the bridge to St. David's Bay. That's where she always goes. Maybe I should call her mother. Get them on the lookout. Mrs. Harding will hate me even more for it but not as much as she will when Miranda tells them what I've done.

The car finally turns over. I gun it down the driveway and onto the main road, a winding, twisting artery that leads to the M-8

"Fuck!" I scream, banging my fist repeatedly on the wheel as my self-hatred chokes me. "Fuck!"

Why did I pick tonight to say anything?

Why did I have to go into London last weekend?

Why did I have to choose this?

Why did it have to choose me?

I'm asking myself a million questions why, hating myself for letting it go this way, wishing dearly that I had done things differently.

I'm asking myself things I don't have any answers to other than:

Because I love Natasha.

It always comes down to that terrible truth.

I love her.

So much.

Too much.

Enough to make me throw everything away.

Because I could no longer live the lie.

It's just that the truth doesn't just hurt, it destroys.

The road twists sharply to the left as it skirts along Braeburn Pond and, in the pouring rain, the wipers going faster and faster, I nearly miss it.

But it's impossible not to.

The broken fence along the side of the road.

The steam rising from beyond the bank.

From where a car has gone over the edge.

A car has gone over the edge.

I slam on my brakes, the car skidding a few feet, and pull to the side of the road.

I don't let the thoughts enter my head.

The thoughts that tell me this is them.

This could be them.

But if it is them, one thought says. *You have to save them.*

I can save them.

I don't know how I manage to swallow that panic down but I do.

I get out of the car, rain in my face.

The air smells like burned asphalt.

The pond is whipped up by the storm.

And as I approach the edge of the road, I can see the faint beam of headlights from down below, a misplaced beacon in the dark.

I look down.

The world around me swims.

The hood of the sedan smashed into a willow tree, the same hood I had my hands on minutes ago, begging her not to leave.

The car is at an angle, leaning on its broken nose.

The steam rises.

And yet I still have hope.

I have to have hope.

I cry out, making noises I can't control, maybe I'm yelling for them, maybe I'm yelling for help. I stumble down the hillside to the car.

Praying.

Praying.

Praying.

They're going to be okay.

They're going to be okay.

The windshield is completely shattered, the sides of jagged glass bordered with red.

I stare stupidly at the empty car.

Then turn my head.

To the space in front of the hood.

And the grass between the car and the pond.

Where two bodies lay, dark in the night.

Two bodies, one big, one small.

Both broken.

Both motionless.

I have one moment of clarity as the truth sinks in.

My truth.

This real truth.

And in that moment I wish to grab the jagged piece of glass lying at my feet.

Put it in my throat.

And end it before I can feel it.

But that would be the coward's way out.

So I stumble forward.

Vomit down my shirt.

Paralysis of the heart.

I cry.

Scream.

Noises animals make.

I stumble past Miranda.

To Hamish.

Fall to my knees.

And cradle my truth in my arms.

And I feel it.

I'll never stop feeling it.

The rain.

The death.

The end of everything.

My world goes black.

And stays that way.

CHAPTER ONE

Brigs

Present time

Pop.

A cork flies off a bottle of alcohol-free champagne. The shit isn't Dom Perignon but for the sake of my brother and his alcohol recovery program, it will do. Besides, it's not what we're drinking that counts – it's what we're celebrating.

"Congratu-fucking-lations, brother," I tell Lachlan, grabbing his meaty shoulder and giving it a rather rough squeeze. I'm beaming at him, conscious of my all-too-wide grin in his face, but I'm happier than I've been in a while. Maybe it's the real champagne I had with our mum before Lachlan and his girlfriend came over.

Wait. Not girlfriend.

Kayla is his fiancé now. And if you ask me, it's about time.

Lachlan nods, smiling wanly in acute embarrassment, which only makes me want to embarrass him more. That's the job of an older brother after all and since our family adopted him when I was out of high school, I missed out on those important torture years of childhood that most siblings experience at the hands of each other.

My mum comes over and pours the non-champagne into our glasses, then into Kayla's who is standing dutifully at Lachlan's side. As usual, she's hanging onto Lachlan in some way – hand at the small of his back – and her cheeks are flushed with emotion. I almost wish she would cry so I could poke fun at her later. She's such a feisty, smart-mouthed girl that a little vulnerable emotion would be wonderful to exploit.

"Here's to Lachlan and the future Mrs. McGregor," my mum says, raising her glass to the happy couple. Before she's about to clink the glasses, she eyes my father who is standing at the edge of the room, poised to take a picture. He's been poised for the last few minutes. "Well, hurry Donald and get over here."

"Right," he says, snapping one more pic of us with glasses in the air and them comes hurrying over. She hands him his glass and we all clink them together.

"Welcome to the family, Kayla," I tell her sincerely. I glance quickly at Lachlan before I add, "I've been bugging him from day one to propose to you, you know. Can't believe it took him so long, especially with a girl like you."

The permanent line between Lachlan's brow deepens, his jaw tense. I think I'm the only person alive that can piss him off and not get scared of him. My brother is giant beast of a man, all beard and muscle and tattoos, and has most recently become the captain of the Edinburgh Rugby team. You don't want to mess with him, unless your name is Brigs McGregor.

"Brigs," my mother admonishes.

"Oh, I know," Kayla says smoothly before taking a sip of her drink. "I'd be lying if I hadn't been leaving out my rings on the dresser, just so it would be easier for him to get the right size."

"That a girl," I tell her and clink her glass again and though I'm suddenly hit by a fleeting memory, about picking out a ring for Miranda, I swallow it down with the bubbles. That's how I've learned to deal with the past – you acknowledge it and move on.

Move on.

Yesterday we were all at the rugby match between Edinburgh and Munster, cheering our arses off. Of course we weren't just there for Lachlan. He had told us a few weeks before that he was going to propose during the game and it would be nice to have the family there. Even though I just started teaching the week before, I flew up from London to Edinburgh on Friday night. Naturally it was hard for me to keep my mouth shut about the event, but I'm glad I did because it made the moment even greater, especially when Lachlan briefly buggered the proposal part up. Naturally it still ended up being romantic as hell.

"This is so exciting," my mum squeals. I don't think I've seen her squeal in a long time. She places her flute on the coffee table and claps her hands together, her bracelets jangling. "Have you given any thought to where the wedding is going to be? When? Oh and the dress. Kayla, darling, you're going to look so beautiful."

I want to keep the grin on my face. I really do. But it's starting to falter.

Move on, move on, move on.

The memories of my mother and Miranda going dress shopping. How long they took – months – before they found the perfect one. How Miranda squirreled that dress home, hiding it in the closet and forbidding me to look at it.

I kept my word. I did. And on our wedding day, she really did take my breath away.

I wish that memory could be pure. I wish that I could grieve like any normal man would do. Feel the sorrow and not the shame.

But all I feel is shame. All I feel is shame.

All my fault.

The thought races through my head, lightning on the brain.

All my fault.

I close my eyes and breathe in slowly through my nose, remembering what my therapist had taught me.

Move on, move on, move on.

It wasn't my fault.

"Brigs?" I hear my father say and I open my eyes to see him peering at me curiously. He gives me a quick, encouraging smile. "Are you all right?" He says this in a low, hushed voice and for that I'm grateful. My mother and Kayla are talking wedding plans, not noticing.

Lachlan, on the other hand, is watching me. He knows my triggers just as I know his. But while we can drink alcohol-free champagne for his sake, we can't ignore fucking life for mine. We can't pretend that love and marriage and babies don't happen, just because all of mine were taken away.

All my fault.

I exhale and paste on a smile. "I'm fine," I say to my father. "Guess I'm a wee bit stressed about classes tomorrow. This will be the first real week of school. The first one never counts for anything. Everyone's lost or hungover."

He gives a little laugh. "Yes, I remember those days." He finishes the champagne and checks his watch, managing to spill leftover droplets on the carpet as he turns his wrist. "What time is your flight tonight?"

"Ten p.m.," I tell him. "I should probably go upstairs and make sure I have everything."

I make for the stairs as Lachlan calls after me, "I'll drive you to the airport."

"No worries," I say. I can tell from the intensity in his eyes that he wants to talk. And by that, he wants me to talk. The last year, leading up to my new job at Kings College and the move to London, Lachlan was on me to make sure I was handling things, that I was doing okay. Maybe it's because I helped him get help for his drug and alcohol addiction, maybe he's just more aware of me in general, as a brother and as a friend.

Our relationship has always been a bit strained and rocky, but at least now he's one of the few people I can count on.

"It's not a problem," he says gruffly, the Lachlan brand of tough love. "I'll drop off Kayla at home, then take you over."

I exhale and nod. "Sure, thank you."

I quickly go upstairs and make sure my overnight bag is in order. When I'm in Scotland I usually stay in my old room at my parents. Makes me feel terribly old, staring down at my old bed, let alone trying to sleep in it, but there's something comforting about it.

My flat in Edinburgh city is being rented at the moment, so there's no staying there – eventually I'll probably sell it. I accepted my position as professor of film studies at the university with a grain of salt with no real long-term commitment. I'm renting a nice flat in the Marylebone area now but until I feel like this job is solid and I'm in for the long-haul, I'm treating my new life with delicate hands.

"How is Winter?" Lachlan asks me later after I've said my goodbyes to my parents and Kayla and we're in his Range Rover, lights flashing past us on the A-90.

"He's a handful," I tell him, tapping my fingers along the edge of the door. "And a right bugger sometimes. And I'm pretty sure my neighbors will file a complaint when he barks again in the middle of the night."

"He's not even a year old yet," Lachlan says. "Give it time. He's still a puppy."

"Aye. He's a shitting machine is what he is."

Lachlan's a dog expert and a dog rescuer. When he's not being a hotshot rugby player, he operates a rescue shelter for dogs, especially pit bulls, and tries to build awareness for them. Kayla works for him and so far the organization has been doing really well. He's the reason why I adopted Winter to begin with. I found the puppy last Christmas during a snow storm by our grandpa's house in Aberdeen, hiding out in the neighbor's barn. When the neighbors wouldn't claim the dog, it was either I take the white fluffball in or Lachlan would take it to his shelter. The bloody dog grew on me, I guess, and now he's a royal pain in the arse who looks like he strolled off the set of Game of Thrones. Still, life would be pretty boring without him, even though I have to hire a dog walker to deal with his excess energy when I'm at school.

"You know," Lachlan says quietly after a few moments. "If any of this gets difficult for you…you can just tell me to shut up. I'll understand."

I glance at him, face half-covered by shadows. "If what gets difficult?"

He clears his throat and gives me an expectant look. "You know. Kayla and I. Getting married. I know it can't be easy…you and Miranda…"

I ignore the icy grip in my chest and try to relax my shoulders. "She's dead, Lachlan. There is no use pretending otherwise and no point in dancing around it." I look back out the window, getting lost in the darkness and beams of passing headlights. "Life is always going to go on, that's what I've learned and I'm making peace with it. Just because some things ended for me, it doesn't mean it ends for everyone else. You're going to marry Kayla and the wedding is going to be beautiful. After that, I'm sure she'll pop out some giant beast-like children. In no way am I not going to want to talk about it, be there for you, and enjoy it. Life goes on, so will I. And so I do. Your life and love and happiness isn't going to stop because of the things I lost. Neither Miranda or Hamish would have wanted that."

Silence fills the car and I can feel him staring at me in that unnerving way of his. I don't turn my head. I just let my words be.

"But it's not just that," he says cautiously. "I can see it in your eyes Brigs. I always have. You're haunted. And it's not by sadness or sorrow. And it's not by Miranda or Hamish. You're haunted by yourself. When will you finally tell me…why? What really happened?"

I swallow hard.

Move on, move on.

Headlights. Street lamps. Everything is growing brighter. The airport is close.

"Lachlan, I liked you better when you didn't talk so much," I tell him, keep my eyes focused on those lights. I make a point of counting them as the zip past. I make a point of not thinking about his question.

I hear him scratch his beard in thought.

"I don't get any complaints from Kayla," he says.

I roll my eyes, happy to have something else to latch onto. "You couldn't do any wrong in that woman's eyes. That's love, mate. And honestly, I'm truly happy you have it. You deserve love most of all."

A few moments pass. "You know," he says, "we're not going to have any."

I glance at him. "Have any what?"

"Kids," he says. He shakes his head. "We discussed it but…she's not sold on the idea and to be honest, neither am I. A kid with my genes…isn't very fair."

I have to say, I'm surprised to hear Lachlan say this, only because of the intensity of his love for Kayla. On the other hand, I'm not surprised to hear her stance on it. Kayla has all the maternal instincts of a rattlesnake. I mean that in the nicest way.

"Well, that's too bad," I tell him, "because genes or no genes, I think you'd make a wonderful father. A far better one than I ever was, that's for sure." I sigh, pinching my eyes shut for a moment. When I open them, we're pulling up to the airport. "But you do what is right for you. If you don't want them, don't have them. The last thing the world needs is another child that wasn't wanted. You and Kayla have your dogs and each other and very busy lives. It's enough. Believe me."

"I'm pretty sure Jessica is going to lose her mind when she finds out," Lachlan says, calling our mother by her name as he usually does. He pulls the car to the Departures curb. "I'm her last chance at grandchildren."

"She had a grandchild," I snap, the words pouring out like poison. My blood thumps loudly in my ears. "His name was Hamish."

Images of Hamish fly past me. Ice blue eyes, reddish brown hair. A big smile. Always asking "Why? Why dada?" He was only two when he was taken from me. He would be nearly six years old now. I always looked forward to him getting into school, I knew his curiosity would lead him to bigger and better things. Though I wasn't in love with Miranda at the end, I was in love with my boy. And even when I had the selfish nerve of dreaming of a different life for myself, he was always my first concern.

It wasn't supposed to happen that way.

Lachlan is staring at me wide-eyed, remorse wrinkling his brow. "Brigs," he says, voice croaking. "I'm sorry. I'm sorry, I didn't mean it."

I quickly shake my head, trying to get the anger out of me. "It's fine, it's fine. I'm sorry. I just...I know what you meant. It's been a long day and I just need to go home and get some sleep."

He nods, frowning in shame. "I get it."

I exhale loudly and then try to perk up. "Well, time to get in through security hell. Thanks for the ride, Lachlan." I reach over into the backseat and bring forward my bag before getting out of the car.

"Brigs," he says again before I close the door, leaning across the seat to look at me. "Seriously. Take care of yourself in London. If you need anything for any reason, just call me."

The fist in my chest loosens. I'm a grown man. I wish he didn't worry so much about me. I wish I didn't feel like I needed it.

I give him a wave and go on my way.

***

All the radio announcers keep yammering on about is how beautiful the weekend was, a real extended summer with record-breaking temperatures and searing sunshine. Of course it happens on the weekend I'm in Scotland and of course as I get ready for this Monday, it's pissing buckets outside.

I eye myself in the hallway mirror and give myself a discerning once-over. I'm wearing a suit today, steel grey, light grey shirt underneath, no tie. Last week was all about making the students feel comfortable – I was in dress shirts and jeans, T-shirts and trousers, but this week is about making the crackdown. Shit. Some of the students in my classes are my age, so I've got to at least look like I mean business, even though I've got dog hair on my shoulders.

My gaze travels to Winter sitting on the floor by the couch, thumping his tail when we make eye contact, and back to the mirror. He's calm for now, but when I leave I know he's going to treat my flat like a gymnasium. Thank god for Shelly, my dog walker.

I smooth back my hair, wearing it fairly short these days, and peer at the grey strands at my temples. Thankfully I've put all my weight back on, so I don't look like the weakling I did before. I've been at the gym most mornings, working hard all summer to get back into shape and it's finally paying off. After the accident and my consequent meltdown (or, as my old job called it before they let me go, my "mental diversion," as if what happened to me could be so neatly explained, like a detour on the road), I wasn't eating. I wasn't living. It wasn't until I found the courage to see a doctor, to get help and finally stay with it, that I crawled out from the ashes.

I'd like to say it all feels like a blur to me, the years at the bottom of the spiral, the world around me bleak, guilt and hatred sticking to me like tar. But I remember it all vividly. In horrible, exquisite detail. Maybe that's my punishment, my shackles for my crimes.

I knew that falling in love was a crime.

I deserve all the punishment I get.

And what's worst of all is how on some nights, the darkest ones when I feel how alone I really am, how badly my choices have tipped the world on its axis, I think about her.

Not Miranda.

I think about *her*.

Natasha.

I think about the reason my judgement became skewed, the reason why I chose my own personal happiness over my family's. I think about the first time I really fell in love. It wasn't a stumble into comfort and complacency, like it had been with Miranda. It was cliff-jumping without a parachute, bungy-jumping with no cord. I knew, I knew, the moment I laid my eyes on Natasha, that I was gone and there wasn't a single thing to hold me in place.

You'd think that memories of love would feel just like the real thing but these memories never feel anything like love. Love is good. Love is kind. Patient. Pure.

So they say.

Our love was a mistake from the start. A beautiful, life-rendering mistake.

Even if I did let myself remember – feel – what it was like to look into her eyes, to hear those words she once so softly whispered, it would do me no good. That love destroyed so much. It destroyed me and I let it tear me apart, willingly. And then I destroyed every last good thing in my life.

Memories of love are a poison.

My therapist told me that I have to embrace it. Acknowledge that people fall in love all the time with people they aren't supposed to, that I was swept away and lost control for once in my life and no matter what, I can't blame myself for Miranda and Hamish's death. It was bad timing. It was an accident. People get divorced every day and it doesn't end that way. Above all, it wasn't my fault.

It's just hard to believe that when none of it would have happened if I hadn't let myself fall in love with another woman. It wouldn't have happened had I not told

Miranda that night, wanting a divorce. They'd still be alive. And I wouldn't be the archaic ruins of a man.

And Natasha is gone, even if the memories remain. In my deep, near suicidal grief, I told her that we had been a mistake and this was our punishment. I told her I never wanted to see her again.

It's been four years now. She's listened.

I sigh and observe my expression. I do seem haunted, as Lachlan says. My eyes seem colder, iceberg blue, the dark shadows at the corner. Lachlan doesn't know the truth though, only my therapist does. Natasha is a secret, a lie, to everyone else.

I paste on a smile that looks more like a wolf's grin, straighten my shoulders and walk out the door, umbrella and briefcase in hand.

My flat is on Baker Street, right across from the Sherlock Holmes Museum. In fact, when I'm particularly despondent, I can spend a few hours just watching the tourists lining up to go inside. One of the reasons I picked the flat was the novelty of this – growing up, I was a huge fan of Holmes, as well as anything Sir Arthur Conan Doyle cooked up. I'm also quite fond of the pub next door. It's a great place to pick up women tourists and if they've just come from the museum, then you know they at least have some kind of brain on them.

Not that I've shared more than a few drinks with these girls – I'm mainly there for the company. Sometimes it ends in the bedroom though often times they go on their merry drunk way and I'm ever the gentleman, the man she'll text her friends about and say "Scottish men are so well-mannered, he bought me a drink and didn't expect anything." The truth is, I'm not ready for dating. I'm not ready for relationships. I'm barely ready for this job.

But you are ready, I tell myself as I dodge the rain and head down into the Tube, taking the passageway across to my line. This week I will set the goals for the semester, this week I'll let the students know what to expect. This week I'll finally start working on my book, *"The Tragic Clowns": Comedic Performance in Early American Cinema.*

As my thoughts jumble together I realize the train is about to close its doors. I do a half-hearted run toward in then stop dead in my tracks.

There is a woman on the train, her back to the closing doors.

I can't see what she's wearing, dark shoulders, maybe a coat.

Her hair is thick, half-wet, honey blonde and trailing halfway down her back.

There's nothing about this girl that says I should recognize her. Know her.

Yet somehow I do.

Maybe not as a blonde, but I swear I do.

I walk right up to the doors as the train pulls away, staring like a madman as it roars down into the dark tunnel, willing for the woman to turn her head even a little bit. But I never see her face and then she's gone and I'm standing on the edge of the platform, left behind.

"Next train shouldn't be long," a man says from behind me, strolling past with a newspaper in his hand.

"Aye," I say absently. I run my hand over my head, shaking sense into me.

It wasn't her.

How can you know someone by the back of their head?

Because you spent months memorizing every inch of her that you couldn't touch, I think. *Your eyes did what your hands and mouth and dick couldn't.*

I exhale and stroll away from the edge. The last thing I need is to start the week like this, looking for ghosts where there aren't any.

I wait for the next train, get off at Charring Cross as usual and walk to school.

CHAPTER TWO

Natasha

Four years ago

"Natasha, do you have a moment? There's a Brigs McGregor here to see you."

"Brigs who?" I ask into the phone. "Is that a first name?" The line crackles and I can barely hear my supervisor Margaret. That's what they get for sticking me in a closet upstairs and calling it an office. Obviously they were so eager to have an intern here, busting her ass and working for free, they'd make an office out of anything. I'm grateful I don't have to type on a toilet.

"Just come downstairs," Margaret says before hanging up the phone.

I sigh and blow a wayward strand of hair out of my eyes. I'm piled knee-deep in script submissions which should have been the highlight of this job but since 90%

of these submissions for the short film festival suck, my days have been come exceedingly tedious.

When I first applied for the internship for the Edinburgh Short Film Festival, I thought it would be a good way to get extra experience before heading into my final year of my Masters degree, especially as I'm targeting my thesis toward the influence of festivals on feature films, or something to that nature anyway. I also thought getting out of London for the summer and checking out Edinburgh would be a nice change of pace, especially from all the dickheads I keep hanging around with at school.

And while I guess those things are true – I am getting good material for my thesis and I am loving Edinburgh – I didn't expect to be the company's little slave girl. Not that I'm little, not with these hips and ass that can barely fit in this damn closet-cum-office, but I'm literally running around from eight in the morning to seven at night and sometimes I think I'm doing the whole show by myself. For example, now they've put me on script submissions for the contest they have going (winning script gets all the equipment to shoot it) and expect me to pick the winner. While I'm flattered with the responsibility, I'm not sure it should fall into my hands.

I'm also not surprised there's some man here to see me, because any time a filmmaker comes in with a proposal or a question or wanting to work with us somehow, they always shuffle them off to see me. I've only been here for three weeks and yet I'm supposed to act like I know everything.

Luckily, I'm pretty good at acting. I mean, at least back in Los Angeles I was.

I get up and leave the office, walking down the narrow hall with its rock walls and wood floors, before going down the stairs to the main level and reception where Margaret is busy typing on her computer. She stops her flying fingers and nods at the seats by the door, below the range of shitty movie posters.

"This is Professor McGregor from the university," she says before going back to work.

A man stands up from the seats and smiles at me.

He's tall, broad-shouldered in a black dress shirt and jeans.

Handsome as hell, all cut jaw with the right amount of stubble, high cheekbones and piercing blue eyes.

The kind of handsome that depletes your brain cells.

"Hello," he says, walking toward me with his hand out.

His smile is blinding white and absolutely devilish.

"Brigs," he says to me as I place my hand in his.

His grip is warm, strong.

"You must be Natasha," he goes on.

Right. This is the part where I speak.

"Y-yes," I stammer and immediately curse myself for sounding less than poised. "Sorry I was distracted by…Brigs, you say. That's an interesting name."

That's an interesting name? Man, I'm winning today.

But he laughs and that smile grows wider.

"Yes, well my parents obviously had high hopes for me. Listen, can I have a minute of your time?"

I glance over at Margaret. "Sure. Margaret, is there a room free?"

She shakes her head, not looking up. Usually I have meetings in any of the other offices.

"Okay, well then." I give Brigs an apologetic look. "Follow me. We'll have to use my office and I apologize ahead of time because it's literally a closet. They keep me like Rapunzel up there."

I walk down the hall and up the stairs, shooting him a glance over my shoulder to make sure he's following me. I expect him to be looking at my ass because it's pretty much in his face and it's the largest thing in the building, but instead he's looking right at me, as if he was expecting to meet my eyes.

"Here we are," I tell him when we reach the top, stepping inside my office and squeezing between the edge of the desk and the wall. I sit down on my chair with a sigh.

"Wow, you weren't kidding," he says, hunched over so his head doesn't smash into the ceiling. "Is there maybe a bucket I could sit on?"

I jerk my head at the stool that's currently covered by scripts. "If you want to pass me those scripts."

He starts piling my desk with them and takes a seat, long legs splayed.

I peer at him over the pile and give him my most charming smile. I really wish I had bothered to look at myself in the mirror before meeting him. I probably have kale in my teeth.

"So how can I help you Professor McGregor."

"Brigs." That smile again.

"Brigs," I say, nodding. "Oh and let me preface our conversation but letting you know I am an intern and I've only been here three weeks and I don't know what I'm doing."

"An intern?" he asks, rubbing his hand along his jaw. "Not from my program."

"I go to school in London."

"Kings College?"

"No, I wish. I couldn't afford it."

"Ah, international student fees. Are you Canadian? American?"

"You mean I don't sound British?" I joke. "I'm American. And yeah, the fees were too much, even though I have a French passport from my father's side, though that only went through this year. Anyway, I'm rambling. Sorry. I go to Met for film. It was *slightly* cheaper."

He nods. "Fine school."

"That's a very diplomatic teacher answer."

"And I'm a diplomatic teacher."

God, to have a student teacher affair with him. Though, I'm 28 and he can't be more than 35, so it wouldn't be all that scandalous and…

My thoughts trail off when I catch sight of his wedding ring for the first time.

Oh.

Well, that figures.

Still, I can stare at him, married or not.

"So what brings you here?" I manage to say.

"Well, it's funny," he says, running his hand through his mahogany hair. "I came here for one reason and now I have two."

I raise my brows. "Okay."

"One reason is that our program at school has trouble competing with the bigwigs down in London, so we decided that perhaps sponsorship of the film festival would give us the right exposure at the right place. In the end, there can only be so many winners and when the festival is over and the failed filmmakers want to throw in their hat, that's when we want to steal them, take advantage of their low self-esteem and bring them to our program."

I purse my lips. "That's a very pessimistic way of looking at things."

"I'm a realist," he says brightly.

"An opportunist."

"Same thing."

Well, we could actually use some more sponsors.

"All right, well I'll have to run this past Margaret and Ted, but I think this is something we'd like to work with you on. What's the other thing?"

"You come work for me."

"Excuse me?"

He looks around the closet office, squinting his eyes at a wet spot on the ceiling where it leaks when it rains (and it rains all the time. I actually do have a bucket in my office just for that). "You seem like a bright girl. I'm starting to write my book and I need a research assistant."

"You're an author?"

"No, not yet," he says, looking away briefly. "But that's what professors do in their spare time, you know. Academic papers, journals. Always writing. Honestly, I'm feeling the pressure but I can't do it on my own. I'm such a slow writer to begin with and anything extra bogs me down."

"What's your book about?"

"Tragic clowns. Buster Keaton, Charlie Chaplin. Their performances in early cinema."

Could this man be any more perfect? I'm freaking obsessed with Keaton, Chaplin, Laurel and Hardy, Harold

Lloyd, all of them, ever since my father got me watching them when I was little. Shit, it's tempting. Really tempting. But Professor Blue Eyes is barking up the wrong tree.

"I'm flattered, I think," I tell him, "but there's no way I could handle two jobs. I literally work here all day long. The intern life. No breaks, no fun."

"You'll only have to work a few hours a day for me, if you like, and if you want more work, that's fine too, and I'll pay you forty pounds an hour. And I'll make sure it can go on your resume."

Forty pounds an hour? To do research on Buster Keaton?

It's like a real dream job landed on my lamp. And a job at that, not a payless internship.

But I can't exactly leave the film fest high and dry either.

"Can I talk it over with the people here?" I ask him. "Maybe we can work something out."

"Of course," he says, giving me a sly smile, like he already knows I'll be working for him. He stands up and puts his business card on the pile of scripts. "When you have an answer about both questions, give me a call." He peers down at me with a tilt of his head. "It was nice meeting you Natasha."

Then he's ducking out the door and he's gone.

THE LIE

Their love led to a lie.

Their truth led to the end.

Scottish enigma Brigs McGregor is crawling out from the ashes. After losing his wife and son in a car accident - and, subsequently, his job - he's finally moving forward with his life, securing a prestigious teaching position at the University of London and starting a new chapter in the city. Slowly, but surely, he's pushing past the guilt and putting his tragic past behind him.

Until he sees her.

Natasha Trudeau once loved a man so much she thought she'd die without him. But their love was wrong, doomed from the start, and when their world crashed around them, Natasha was nearly buried in the rubble. It took years of moving on to forget him, and now that she's in London, she's ready to start over again.

Until she sees him.

Because some loves are too dangerous to ever rekindle.

And some loves are too powerful to ignore.

Can you ever have a second chance at a love that ruined you?